T0129144

After The Laughter

Also by Ronald E. Kimmons

An Infinity of Interpretations
A Bit of Social Commentary on and a Philosophical
Examination of Life in These Times

After The Laughter

A Novel

Ronald E. Kimmons

AFTER THE LAUGHTER
A NOVEL

iUniverse books may be ordered through booksellers or by contacting:

iUniverse
1663 Liberty Drive
Bloomington, IN 47403
www.iuniverse.com
1-800-Authors (1-800-288-4677)

Because of the dynamic nature of the Internet, any web addresses or links contained in this book may have changed since publication and may no longer be valid. The views expressed in this work are solely those of the author and do not necessarily reflect the views of the publisher, and the publisher hereby disclaims any responsibility for them.

Any people depicted in stock imagery provided by Thinkstock are models, and such images are being used for illustrative purposes only. Certain stock imagery © Thinkstock.

ISBN: 978-1-4917-8847-9 (sc)
ISBN: 978-1-4917-8927-8 (hc)
ISBN: 978-1-4917-8883-7 (e)

Library of Congress Control Number: 2016931753

Print information available on the last page.

iUniverse rev. date: 02/11/2016

DEDICATION

To

Michele J. Pitman
My friend, lover, and confidante who offered encouragement to me in writing this book and provided feedback on a first draft

The late Betty L. Richards
Who was an inspiration to me on how to live a life well

Vicki and Cydney
My daughters and the true loves of my life

Erin and Arthur (III)
My grandchildren and the other true loves of my life

Arthur, Jr.
Their father

My parents and siblings—Bertram, Donald, Wally Rose, Wayne, Frank, Mildred, Herbert, Exzene, Talmadge, Eugene, Jr., Eugene, and Alberta Always there to support me in whatever I was doing—what a great family

CONTENTS

CHAPTER ONE

Joy and Pain

Most of what you can get in life can be gotten through deception. Almost all of what you can keep comes only through transparency. That's a lesson about life that did not come from his father. It was a lesson that he had somehow put together over the many decades he had been in this world. But it was only during that last summer that it became so clear. That last summer was filled with more beauty and delight than he had ever known and embraced. He did not understand how or why it was happening that way.

Most of the lesson he had learned so well came from the joy he had known and the pain he had endured from the various women he had known over the years. Women he had run from, chased, courted, befriended, made love to, loved, left, and married. Women he had revered, adored, and idolized. Through all of it, he had never met a woman he could completely trust, and that included the first real love of his life and the last.

That last summer began at a 50th Anniversary Reunion of his high school graduation class. There he ran into Jackie, the youngest sister of his first real love. Jackie was a petite, cute woman, reminiscent of her sister, Juliet. He and Jackie somehow had been assigned to the same table for that affair at the beginning of the summer of 2009. When he sat down next to Jackie, he immediately noticed the slit in the middle of her long evening gown that went all the way up to her middle thigh. He was inclined to linger but looked away because he had a vision of her as a young girl peeping from behind a curtain watching him and her sister make out in the living room of her home.

As a young man, he lived in an area in Chicago known as Armour Square, part of a larger area in Chicago known as Bronzeville on the South Side of Chicago. As he would learn later, for the most part, Bronzeville was inhabited by Blacks that came to Chicago as part of the First Great Migration. Then, as now, that area of Chicago was mostly known because of two names: Comiskey Park (aka Cellular Field) and The Illinois Institute of Technology.

He knew the area well because, as a young boy, he attended Robert S. Abbott Elementary School on 37th and Wells streets, just two blocks south of Comiskey Park. During the summer, he and two of his brothers would sell scorecards and newspapers for day and evening games at that park. After they finished selling scorecards and newspapers, they would play a cat-and-mouse game with policemen to see if they could sneak into the game without paying for a ticket. They seldom got caught; and even when the policemen caught them, they usually were just made to sit in the paddy wagon until the game was over.

He learned a lot about The Illinois Institute of Technology because he had always thought about going to college there. From his viewpoint, it never made sense to go hundreds of miles or even five miles away to school when there was one less than three-quarters of a mile away from where he lived. He never fully knew why that was an aspiration for him as a young man because nobody in his family had been to college. But early in his life, he had heard the name Ludwig Mies van der Rohe, one of the giants of modern-day architecture and almost a god in Chicago, and that name and the proximity of the place where Mies taught acted like magnets for him.

His family resided in a two-story apartment building on South LaSalle Street, now barely referenced by a streetlight pole on the northbound ramp of the Dan Ryan Expressway. Jackie's house, by contrast, was unlike any house that he had seen. Her house was in another area of Bronzeville in Chicago not too far from the lakefront and close to a public housing project known as Ida B. Wells. Jackie's house was a three-story, Greystone on the near southeast side of Chicago, unusual because it was a single-family dwelling owned and occupied by only one African-American family. In fact, the entire block was composed of similar dwellings all owned by Black families.

As a young man, he remembered hearing stories about life in the Bronzeville area of Chicago in the good old days. He also remembered seeing pictures of his parents and older siblings in bars and clubs and other places in different areas of Bronzeville. He had also heard stories about how Bronzeville, in its heyday, had many attractions and celebrities: nightclubs such as the Club Delisa, Savoy, Sunset Cafe, and Dreamland Cafe; dance halls such as Warwick Hall and the Forum; concert venues, such as the Regal Theater; writers such as Richard Wright and Gwendolyn Brooks; and musicians such as Louis Armstrong and Nat "King" Cole.

As he sat and chatted with Jackie, his mind drifted away from their conversation, and he went back to the day he first met her sister. He met Juliet the first day he went to high school. That first day in high school was intimidating. But there she was, and she was comforting. He remembered this girl who, with her head tilted to the left and slightly looking down and sideways, kept staring at him the whole time they were in homeroom.

As homeroom ended, the girl who had been watching him walked up to him and said: "Hi. This invitation is for a party I want you to attend on Friday night at my house. I like the way you look."

He took the piece of paper that had printed on it a name, address, time, date, and admission price for the party. He put the paper in his pocket and went to his first-period class. He was excited. Juliet was cute. She had this heart shaped face and bushy eyebrows. She was tall and thin, but she had a great shape and great legs. She had a bob haircut that ended in a V shape at the nape of her neck. She was the first girl that he knew to have that haircut style; and because of the cut, from behind you could see most of her long thin neck, which added to her aura of regality that she already possessed because of her stature and bearing. Her smile was different from that of any girl he had ever met, and she had a weird laugh that made you think of a hyena.

He made the party that Friday night, and it was in this huge house right across the street from the school. As he approached the house, he saw this great stone porch with a small portico and seven steps leading up to it. The door to the house sat open, and the party was on the first floor to the left as soon as he walked in the door and took a few steps into the vestibule.

There were no lights in the place except a red one in a second room behind the one he entered. Real slow music played, a tune by The Platters called "The Great Pretender," and all he could smell and hear were sweaty bodies moving to the music. To him, everyone appeared oblivious to everyone else, and when Juliet touched his neck from behind, he shivered involuntarily.

She didn't say anything but, "Hi," and then lead him to the dance floor.

All of this so aroused him that he could not resist at all. He followed her throughout the night. Wherever she led him, he followed.

He kept thinking: '*She does this so easily, I must be like a young boy to her.*'

And indeed, he was a younger boy if not a young boy in comparison to a lot of other dudes and young ladies in his freshman class. One of his elementary school teachers, Mrs. Eloise Brown, had recommended to the principal that he receive a double promotion at the end of 2nd grade. He often wondered what his life would have been like without that double promotion.

As they danced and moved from one dark corner of the room to another, Juliet kissed him everywhere she could without being outright indecent. He loved it. He took it all in and gave as much as he knew back. The whole evening was like a dream, nothing was material, nothing was real, and everything flowed, effortlessly.

At the end of the evening, Juliet gave him her number and told him to call her. From that point on, they were inseparable; but towards the end of the school year, Juliet started to act a bit funny, and he knew something was wrong. There were times when they wouldn't talk for days at school or over the phone. He didn't know what the problem could be until he saw a senior talking to her in the hall one day. The senior had her pinned against the locker with his body, and she giggled and grinned for days.

The hurt was deep, and he couldn't wait to ask her about it over the phone that evening. She told him that the fellow's name was Trump. He was a captain in the R. O. T. C., and he wanted to take her to the military ball the next week.

He asked her was she going, and she said, "Yes." She thought it was great for a freshman to be able to go out with a senior, especially to the military ball. She said she had her dress picked out and that he was just a nice guy. She quietly added that he didn't mean much to her, just someone who thought enough of her to take her to the military ball.

He asked: "What about me?"

4

She said: "I love you, but I just want to be able to go to the military ball with Trump."

That was not easy for him to take. He felt betrayed. As his first real love, he had not put up any fences around his love or developed any defense against even the possibility of betrayal. He had become unmindful of all of the other young ladies in his world. He worshiped Juliet. He liked the way she made him feel. He even liked the way she made his loins and stomach ache after they petted and kissed for too long.

He knew that her going to the military ball with Trump was more than her just going to the military ball with Trump. He knew that was the beginning of a serious relationship between them. He knew that whatever he meant to her at one time was now overshadowed by this new relationship.

He saw her many times after that to try to persuade her that he was the one who loved her; the one who cared for her more than any other fellow could care for her; and who wanted her more than anything else.

It did not turn around. He realized each time they talked (and sometimes even kissed and petted) that she had moved on and that he needed to do the same. Gradually, they could just see each other in the hall and just wave. Even then there was a spark between them, but they never tried to do much with that.

In their sophomore, junior, and senior years; she would occasionally see him in the hall or call him on the phone to tell him how much she loved him and what a mistake it was for her to get involved with Trump. She never asked for them to get back together, but she always wanted him to know that if he wanted that, she would be open to it.

They didn't get back together. He had moved on. Still, there was this excitement stirring in him whenever he thought about her, especially the Friday night they first danced and their bodies locked in a sweet and trembly embrace.

He stood up and looked at Jackie, and said: "Let's Dance."

CHAPTER TWO

Old Places And Familiar Faces

As he danced with Jackie, he was tempted to pull her up close and hold her as he had done with her sister. But the image of her peeping from behind the curtain kept coming back to him. So he kept his embrace of her a respectable one. On occasion, he did feel her tug at his waist to pull him closer, but he would only allow her to pull him so close. He understood what that was about, and he did not want to give in to the moment. He knew that would be a complicated relationship from her perspective and his. And then the music stopped.

He took her back to the table, held her chair, asked if she wanted a drink, which she declined, and then moved to the bar. There he met an old classmate named Charlotte, and he offered to buy her a drink. She accepted his offer, so they both stood with drinks in hand and talked about the reunion and who was looking like what and who was doing what and to whom.

Charlotte was one of the young ladies who lived in a housing project on 39th (or "tres-nine," as his younger brother called it) and Wentworth Avenue, just across the alley behind his house and to the west. They had known each other for a long time because they had even gone to the same elementary school and their families knew one another. Although he and Charlotte liked each other, in a friendly way, they never had that chemistry lovers have.

He thought about Charlotte and how they had always competed for academic honors in elementary school. That in itself made it difficult for them to be more than just friends. Still, his memories of her were fond ones. What he remembered most about Charlotte was that she had this friend named Francis, who lived about two and a half blocks from where he lived. Francis went to Phillips High School, too, and she was a year ahead of him and Charlotte. How Charlotte and Francis became friends was always a mystery to him.

That did not matter. In the summer after his freshman year of high school and the loss of his first real love, Francis was the antidote he sought to help him get over that time in his life where there were days when he only half ate and got only a little sleep.

Francis was closer to being a woman than a young lady. She was a little taller than Juliet—and a little thicker, as the women use to say in his neighborhood. The men in his neighborhood, young and old, described her as stacked. Juliet was cute, but Francis was beautiful. The young men and older men in his neighborhood called her fine. She had this face that made you just want to kiss it, and she had this body that made you just want to hold it.

If Juliet was regal looking, Francis embodied regality. She wore her hair in long curls that enveloped her face like the faces you saw in pictures and the movies depicting times long gone. She also had this quiet but commanding air about her. When she smiled, her smile did not have the verve that Juliet's had, but it still invited you in.

The first time he had the opportunity to have an extended conversation with Francis was one Sunday afternoon when they ran into each other at a small grocery store on the corner of 39th and Federal. At first, they barely spoke. But she decided to come towards him and have a conversation.

She asked him, "Do you live in the neighborhood?"

He replied, "Yes. On the other side of the tracks on LaSalle Street."

She then asked, "Why are you here at this store instead of the one that is a shorter distance from your house in the opposite direction?"

He had no idea of why he had chosen that store that day, but to keep the conversation going he offered to walk her home and tell her why he chose to come to that store that day. She lived about a block and a half away on the same street as the store, and he knew well the possibility of running into members of street gangs that were just beginning to form at that time.

As they walked, he offered up a little story about how at the age of 3 or 4 he had gone to that same store with his brother and sister, Dwayne and Rosemary; and how his brother and sister walked off and left him at the store. He went on to tell her about how the store owners called the police, and how the policemen took him to the station in a black and white squad car, and how the desk sergeant at the police station gave him his first taste of meat—a baloney sandwich that the sergeant had apparently brought for lunch. She appeared to be amused by his tale, and for the first time she seemed to be relaxed enough to offer up a genuine smile and girl-like giggle.

When they got near her house; she stopped walking, ceased smiling, and seemed reluctant to even let him come close to getting a full view of her house. He knew immediately what the situation was, and he took her hand and held it to gently pull her forward. Her house was a stark contrast to Juliet's. This house was a one-story, wood bungalow with no grass or trees on the outside. The house had the appearance of one that had not been painted in years, and the front porch had a tilt that was immediately noticeable as you approached the stairs to the house.

He had been in that area many times and never paid much attention to what was there until now. To the west were railroad tracks that separated her street from the one he lived on. To the south was another set of tracks that was the beginning of a set of tracks that curved and went west across and through the city to some unknown destinations. Not far from there were L tracks that carried the locals to various parts of the city.

The contrast between who she appeared to be and where she lived was great. It didn't matter to him. He was from a poor family, too, so he sympathized with how she felt. Beyond that, at the moment they stood in front of her house holding hands, his spirits were higher than they had been in quite some time. He knew she was older than him, but he had already decided that they would have a relationship of some kind. His deepest wish was for it to be a romantic relationship.

As she walked into her house, she turned, smiled, and waved goodbye. When he walked towards his house, he did not remember whether or not he had returned her gestures with a smile and a wave. But he did remember exhaling the moment she had closed the door, and a calm came to his soul that he had not known for a bit of time. He also remembered that he had not explained why he was at that store that day, but he understood that while that was an interesting question, the answer did not matter. It was just her way of initiating a conversation. And his answer, as far as he was able to take it, did not matter either. It was just him leaving the house and making a left turn instead of a right turn that brought him to that store.

At that moment, he was not inclined to try to make more of his choice than what was right there on the surface. The heaviness of a past relationship with Juliet had lifted, and the lightness inherent in just the possibilities of a new relationship almost made him giddy. So he took that moment and held on to it as he glided home.

When he got home, his grandmother made an inquiry about what took him so long to go to the grocery store. Initially embarrassed by the question, he did manage to get out that he had walked a girl to her house and that the girl did not live far from the store. His grandmother, a quiet woman, did not press the issue.

She reached her hand out to receive the Crisco shortening that she needed to fry some chicken for the evening meal, and she said, "Boy, be careful out there in them streets," an admonition routinely uttered to boys in his neighborhood during that time. He heard his grandmother but made no reply.

She then told him to prepare the chicken for frying. That was part of the deal for her, especially on Sunday. If you wanted to eat, in some way or another, you had to help prepare the meal. It was as simple as that, and he and all of his siblings—girls and boys alike—knew that that was an expectation held for them by their parents as well as their grandmother.

He felt a tug at his sleeve and realized that Charlotte was trying to get his attention. When he looked at her, she had a knowing smile, and he had the feeling that she had been on the jaunt with him and delighted in it. He extended his elbow, which she quickly took, and they moved back to the table where Jackie still sat. As he approached the table, he felt impetuous; and he asked both Jackie and Charlotte to dance with him at the same time.

He reached for Jackie's hand to help her get up from the table, and as she rose, she had to open her legs a little wider to get a balanced stance. The split in her long dress revealed more of her inner thighs than he had seen before, and this time, he did linger until she noticed him looking. He reflexively moved his head a bit to the left in a futile attempt not to stare, but that was an unsuccessful gesture. A coy smile flashed across her face, but she said not a word. The three of them moved to the dance floor.

The DJ played an old song from the early eighties by a group called Vanity 6. The cut was "Nasty Girl," and all three of them immediately went into this smooth, rhythmic gyration of the hips, and then they moved their legs and feet up and down to keep up with the beat. Then the three moved into a closed circle and continued to move their hips and legs up and down to the beat. Jackie at some point got in front of him, opened wide the split in her dress so she could open her legs and move her body across his. Charlotte was howling and raised her already short skirt so that she could freely move her legs. She then got behind him, real close, and both Jackie and Charlotte laughed as they sandwiched him between them.

He was not embarrassed. It was a groove for him. He moved up closer to Jackie to get his body in between her legs while pulling Charlotte closer to him from behind with his right arm. '*That's intimacy,*' he thought. For a full five minutes, they danced and diaphanously touched each other. When he had asked both ladies to dance with him at the same time, he had no idea of how the three of them would act or interact on the dance floor, but the actual moments were more magical than the thoughts.

This record got more people on the dance floor than any other record that evening, but the dancing crowd clearly enjoyed the antics of the three of them as they merged spirits. They clearly were having fun and enjoying each other, and they obviously did not care who was watching or what they thought. When the record ended, the crowd clapped for both the DJ and the three of them. The three of them laughed and hugged as they left the floor. He thought to himself: '*Man! That was great.*'

As he returned the ladies to their seats, he thought about his first wife, Betty, who knew both Charlotte and Juliet well. Many years ago, he had talked at some point with Charlotte about his relationship with Betty because his youngest sister and Charlotte had been close friends from the old neighborhood in which their families had lived. He had told Charlotte about how as a young man he had gone into therapy because of struggles he was having in his life.

As a young man, one of the incidents that had sent him to therapy was related to a Dear John letter he had received when he was a freshman at the University of Wisconsin in Madison, Wisconsin. The letter was from Betty, a young lady that he had dated steadily during his junior and senior years in high school. After they had graduated from high school, they had plans to go on to college: him to Wisconsin and a planned career as a chemist; her to a local college and a planned career as a high-powered business executive.

As the summer ended and they prepared to go away to college, there was a little distance between them that neither had focused on. In the Dear John letter she sent to him that fall, she told him that somewhere along the way, she got the idea that he was no longer interested in her life, and she wanted to try something new. A few days later he decided to leave the university and join the Army.

He knew that when he left the university, he could be drafted to serve in the armed forces. The Korean War had ended, but there were rumblings of a war in Vietnam. World War II was a recent event in the memory of the country, and America already had troops stationed in Europe, Japan, and Korea when he decided to join the Army. So the prospect of serving somewhere outside of the United States was more than possible; it was probable. He had mixed feelings about that, but he still went to the Armed Forces Recruiting Office at 910 S. Michigan, less than a half mile from where he currently lived.

He hadn't joined the Army just in response to the Dear John letter he got from his high-school sweetheart, although that did bring back memories of the relationship with his first love, Juliet. He joined because he was in an emotional turmoil about his life. The stay at the University of Wisconsin ended badly; terminated mid-semester because he did not receive money that had been promised to him by an organization back in Chicago.

The train ride back to Chicago from Wisconsin was a tearful one, laden with the sense of another lost love and a dream of future success turned upside down. He was in such turmoil that he believed he was having a nervous breakdown.

Betty was a year older and a semester ahead of him in high school. They had met at a Friday night social where he was attempting to perfect dance steps taught to him by his youngest sister and several of her girlfriends. The dance lessons had started at the beginning of his sophomore year in high school; and as he learned how to "Bop" and "Walk," he would attempt to incorporate steps and movements of Fred Astaire when he held Ginger Rogers in his arms and swept her gracefully across the dance floor.

The week following his return to Chicago from the University of Wisconsin, he met Betty for breakfast at Gladys' Luncheonette, a popular soul food restaurant on 45th and Indiana. After breakfast, they went to her apartment. When he told Betty that he had joined the Army, she grabbed him and held him tightly, as if to prevent him from taking a single step. She fell softly onto his right arm and shoulder and sobbed uncontrollably.

He had hoped she would express some regret about his going away, but her sobbing went far beyond anything that he could have imagined. He pulled her to his bosom and held her as tight as he could. The two of them rocked in each other's arms like children trying to console themselves.

After about thirty minutes in that embrace, she let him go. They both then sat down on the floor in her living room, in the front part of an apartment on the second floor of a six-flat on 59th and Indiana. She told him that she wished he wouldn't go but that she understood. He told her he wanted to stay but that he had to go. They agreed not to talk about the future beyond an agreement that they would stay in touch. Then they tearfully embraced and fell silent.

The day he went to the Armed Forces processing center, he was both excited and a little afraid. The recruiters had talked to him and others about the recruitment process, but it was all still abstract to him. From beginning to end, the experience in the processing center was efficient, with little conversation or humane connection. At the end of it all, he and about a hundred young men raised their hands and took the Oath of Enlistment, similar to the oath used to swear in elected officials and judges: "I do solemnly swear that I will support and defend …" That evening he boarded a train to Fort Carson, Colorado to begin his basic training in the United States Army.

CHAPTER THREE

Love and War

As he sat on the train and watched the skyline of the city gradually disappear, he thought about where he might wind up if he were shipped abroad. Not a single option appealed to him. He especially did not want to go to Germany. He wasn't sure how he had gotten those images, but all he could imagine were bombed out buildings where Nazi soldiers hid as they waited to attack American soldiers, especially Black and Jewish soldiers. He thought about being captured and taken to a concentration camp or just disappearing and never being heard from again. He was afraid when he had those thoughts, and that troubled him.

He got a bottle of soda from the bar, and returned to his seat and lit a cigarette. He had smoked cigarettes since he was ten years old, another one of the many things—good and bad—his youngest sister had taught him. The two of them were only a year apart in age; so despite the fact that he had nine brothers, chronologically and socially she was his closest sibling. He smiled as he recalled how they had gone to the alley behind the houses and coal yard across the street and to the east of their house to learn how to smoke.

Looking back, he was hard pressed to understand how he picked up the habit since his early experiences with cigarettes were absolutely horrible. He had coughed and wheezed after every puff, and the burning in his chest was really painful. Still, he had persisted, and now sat comfortably inhaling and exhaling the smoke from the Winston cigarette he held in his right hand. He was sad about leaving Chicago, but he also felt liberated by the prospect of being away from there and all of the things he had lived through and that had defined his existence.

In that moment, he thought about Francis and how that relationship had evolved. After their chance meeting at the grocery store, they did develop a relationship that was strange because she was going with this star basketball player from another high school about two miles south of the school they attended. As for him, he dated and talked to lots of girl from a variety of high schools on the south and west sides of the city. So while the relationship with Francis was a good one, he recognized that he was not central to her life, and they often only met to talk or have sex—in any place they could steal a moment or two of privacy.

She was one of the few young ladies that he knew who smoked, and in that moment on the train, he had images of her sitting across from him at a party, legs crossed and arms resting on her thighs. She held a Kool cigarette in her right hand, and occasionally would take a deep drag and slowly blow the smoke in his direction. Because of the way she sat, whenever she exhaled there was a bit of an upward movement of her right foot and then this stimulating and ample flash of the outer thigh, followed by a coy smile. She had gorgeous legs that were amplified by the yellow, short skirt and black, strapped, open-toe, high-heel shoes she wore.

After a few minutes of watching Francis' beguiling moves; he got up, took a few steps towards her, put out his hand in a gesture to get her to dance with him, took her to the dance floor, and started his Fred Astaire-Ginger Rogers moves. She smiled as they glided around the edges of the room. She told him that he was the only young man she knew that wanted to combine soul music dancing with stuff from Hollywood movies. The disc jockey played a tune by Nat King Cole called "When I Fall in Love" and followed that with a version of the same song by Doris Day. That was an interesting song and combination of records for this setting. His and Francis' bodies intertwined and their lips meshed in a kiss that made his soul levitate.

It was only when he held Francis close that he truly understood what a magnificent body she had. He always thought that Francis had the kind of body that every boy (and man) lusted after and every girl (and woman) wished for. That evening they both had had a little to drink; and the combination of the feel of her body, the smell of alcohol and cigarettes together, and the faint aroma of her perfume made for a heavenly moment that both decided should be honored in some earthly way.

He had an older brother who lived not far from the party and even a shorter distance from Francis' house. He was a little embarrassed when his brother opened the door and saw them standing there holding hands but not saying a word. His brother, Theodore, did not speak either, and merely stepped back to allow them to enter as he pointed to the top of the stairs.

His seat shook a little as the train braked to make its first stop--in Naperville, a town twenty-eight miles west of Chicago. By then, he had started to nod a little. So he clutched his carry-on bag in both arms, laid his head back, and slept for about an hour. Images of Betty floated in and out of his mind. She had decided not to see him off, and he decided that that might have been a defining moment in their relationship. He didn't want to think a lot about it; so he flipped the pages of the Jet and Ebony magazines that he had bought at Union Station in Chicago.

Jet was the magazine he preferred most because it usually had attractive Black women on the cover, sometimes scantily clothed in bathing suits. Jet also featured a centerfold picture of a black woman in a bathing suit each week. He remembered how the guys in his neighborhood always made that the first page they looked at when they got their hands on a copy of Jet. By the time he started to read the Ebony magazine, he was nodding again and drowsily watched the names of towns come and go as the train moved towards Colorado: Princeton, Galesburg, Burlington, Mt. Pleasant, Ottumwa, Osceola, Creston, Omaha, Lincoln, Hastings, Holdrege, McCook, and Fort Morgan.

That was the first time that he had been that far west, and he was pleased that he had the opportunity to see this part of the United States, simply because he had chosen to join the Army. For the first time in his life, he started to understand just how vast this country was. He sighed as he thought about all of the individuals on the South Side of Chicago who not only had not been this far away from Chicago but who also had not been into downtown Chicago. That thought made him sad, so he decided to think about basic training. He did not quite know what to expect in basic training, but he had decided that he would handle it—no matter what.

The train pulled into Denver at 1:50 P.M. It had left Chicago at 7:35 P.M. the day before. It took more than seventeen hours to go a little bit more than a thousand miles across the heartland. To get to their final destination, Fort Carson (near the towns of Colorado Springs and Pueblo), they had to take an old army bus that rattled so much that he and all of the other recruits were sure they would never make it to Fort Carson. But they did, and the next eight weeks were tougher than anything he could have imagined, not the least of which was the requirement that he learn how to make up his bunk bed so that a quarter thrown down on it would bounce high into the air!

The training was arduous—often in inclement weather and at night. There were long marches with heavy backpacks and weapons; and trying to pitch his tent on the side of a mountain while it rained while attempting to keep his weapon dry did stretch him as a person. "Old Reliables," the 9th Infantry Division of the United States Army, conducted the training at Fort Carson. The whole ordeal was hard but bearable. He was very much aware, however, that there were many recruits who just left the training grounds and melted into the civilian population of Colorado Springs or Pueblo. Others were just put on a bus and sent back to Chicago.

Not all of his days there were bad. Some days when they were in the mountains on bivouac, the sun would come out after a bit of rain, and the sun rays could barely be seen between the top of the mountains and the white clouds that seem to touch the peaks of the mountains, especially Pikes Peak. The only word that came to his mind in those moments was "heaven."

At the midpoint of the training, he got a weekend pass and headed to Pueblo just south of Fort Carson. He had no desires other than to be off the post and among civilians. The following weekend he headed north to Colorado Springs. Again, it was like being let out of a cage. He saw a couple of movies, tried out a few restaurants, and talked smack with his buddies. Then they would all catch the last bus back to the camp to avoid the cost of a hotel room.

In the last week of camp, he got his first letter from Betty. He thought to himself, '*What is this?*' He could not believe that she decided to write him after he had been gone for more than seven weeks and he had not heard a word from her. He sat on the side of his bunk bed hesitating to open the letter.

When he finally opened the letter, he saw only a half page of neatly written words: "Hi. I am sorry I was so long in writing. I wanted to take the time to sort out my life and your place in it, if any. I have decided that after you finish your training and receive a permanent assignment, we should get married. I know that sounds strange, but I am having a hard time trying to imagine life without you. Will you at least think about marrying me? Please! Write soon. Love, Betty."

Although he had not felt like crying, a couple of tears did roll down the right side of his face. Initially, he thought about wiping them away; but instead climbed in his bunk bed to just let them dry on his face, laid on his left side, and tried to imagine what a life with Betty might be like. Betty was cute, tall and thin; and she had an allure few others young ladies could match. She was a cheerleader and co-captain of the squad. Just as important, she had entered his life not too long after he met Francis and about six months after he broke up with Juliet.

He and Francis had a very comfortable relationship—you know, "friends with benefits." But both knew that her other relationship with the star basketball player was the one that warmed the cockles of her heart—and perhaps some other places, too. That was okay. Neither could define their relationship and neither ever tried. When he thought about their relationship, he was always in a peaceful and happy place—even in the absence of thoughts about a future and time spent in the past.

He woke up with a little wetness on the left side of his face and the letter from Betty on the floor. Except for a little light coming through the windows of the barracks from the half-moon, the place was completely dark. It was suppertime, so he thought he should hurry and get to the mess hall before it closed. He quickly washed his face, brushed his hair, threw on his fatigues jacket, and rushed out the door. When he got to the mess hall, the feeding line was closing down. The men behind the serving counter just waited until he got a food tray, and each gave him generous helpings of food as he pushed his tray down the three-legged iron rack on the side of the serving table.

He ate alone, as he often did even when he was on time for chow. He liked being alone, and he hated the inane chatter that often took place in the mess hall when he sat with other soldiers. This was his last week of basic training; he had not made a single friendship. And that was almost what was expected. All of the recruits knew that after eight weeks, they would probably never see one another again. They would either go into advanced training in their MOS (military occupational specialty) or get additional training as an infantryman, or foot soldier as some called it. No need to make friends.

Before he left Chicago, the recruiter asked him if he wanted to go to the Army's Officer Candidate School and become a second lieutenant. He considered the offer but decided he did not want the responsibility for another person's life or well-being. That decision would become one of his "almost regrets" when he sometimes thought about what his life might have been like instead of what it was.

He returned to the barracks, which now was well lit and inhabited by twenty other recruits. He thought about Betty and the letter she wrote, but he was not inclined to respond to it. He did think about Francis and whether or not he would have wanted to marry her. Francis had a hold on his heart that made him wistful in that moment. He sat on the side of his bunk and lit a cigarette. He did not smoke a lot, but a cigarette with a drink and after a meal were his favorite times to smoke. Considering that he only smoked four or five cigarettes a day, he often wondered why he smoked at all. It was beyond his comprehension how some recruits would smoke several packs of cigarettes a day!

He took a long drag on his cigarette and pretended to slowly blow the smoke at Francis. In response, she came over, sat next to him, leaned over towards his face, and licked the inside of his ear. He shivered and then noticed his bunk buddy looking down at him from the bed above. He just nodded his head to acknowledge his bunk buddy's presence, lay back in his bed, and lit another cigarette.

He remembered that more than a year ago, he and Francis had parted company on a warm summer evening on the lakefront in Chicago. In a few days, she would head to Spellman College in Atlanta, Georgia. She wanted to become an artist of some sort. The idea of her leaving Chicago to go to school in Atlanta occasionally left him a little confused since the Art Institute of Chicago had one of the best art schools in the world. But it didn't take much additional thought to understand why she wanted to go to school in Atlanta.

As they often did, they merely held hands and sat in silence, occasionally making small talk about things or people they observed: Chicago's marvelous skyline as seen from across the lake in an area near the Shedd Aquarium; the looks they got from Whites, for whatever reason; the white sails of all of the boats on the lake, so that you hardly noticed the boats themselves; Navy Pier, which jutted out into the lake like a finger—formerly a naval training station and then a two-year branch of the University of Illinois, Chicago; the Field Museum of Natural History—best seen and appreciated for its neoclassical architecture when viewed from a moving car in the southbound lanes of Lake Shore Drive; couples of varying hues holding hands and kissing as they walked east and west along the paths leading to and from the Adler Planetarium; Chicago's mounted policemen as they sat on animals as beautiful as any they had seen, even in the movies, all with a similar color—brownish; the azure blue water, low-hanging clouds, and yellowish sky that was visible between the lake and the clouds; and each other—with eyes that almost allowed them to see the soul of the other. He sat up in his bunk and decided that he would answer Betty's letter with a single word: Maybe.

CHAPTER FOUR

Love and Pieces

He was now on an airplane headed back to Chicago. The trip out to Fort Carson on the train was great, but he was not inclined to spend almost a day getting back to a place that he could get to in a little more than three hours by plane. He did not care that the cost of a ticket would be three times that of a train ticket or that this would be his first ride on an airplane. What he wanted was to get back to a place that he had rushed to leave eight weeks ago. When he landed at Midway Airport, his stomach was very upset, and he gagged a little as he stepped from the passenger boarding bridge into the terminal. He was barely able to hold onto his duffle bag as he ran to the nearby washroom.

As he sat in a taxi headed home, he thought about Midway Airport that was on the south side of the city and still the busiest airport in the world. The airport was not too far from where he now lived. Soon after he left Chicago for basic training, his family had moved farther south in the city to an area called Englewood. There was a massive government land grab in that area on the south side where most Blacks lived.

The exercise of eminent domain in this instance, he recalled, centered on efforts to build the Dan Ryan Expressway, a leg of the interstate highway system, which ran through the heart of Chicago. The expressway was originally scheduled to be built close to a part of the city where the mayor lived, but the planned highway was moved east, he was told, to separate the Black population from an area on the south side where the mayor lived.

He had ten days to be at home with his family. Then he would have to go to the Army's Adjutant General School near Indianapolis, Indiana for another eight weeks of training to become a military stenographer. It was strange how he had chosen his military occupational specialty, mostly from the standpoint of what he did not want to become in terms of a job in the Army.

He had rejected becoming an officer based upon his temperament; he could not envision himself as an infantryman—based mostly on what his older brothers had told him about their experiences in that branch of the Army during World War II and the Korean War; and he knew that he was so far beyond some of the other jobs (cooks, orderlies) to which many Blacks had been restricted that those jobs never really crossed his mind.

So when the recruiter showed him a list of occupational specialties, he focused mostly on military stenography because in his senior year in high school his English teacher made him take two semesters of typing because his handwritten essays were extremely difficult to read. In fact, the teacher warned him that he probably would not graduate unless he took typing and typed all of his papers, especially his final term paper.

In addition to refining a skill that he had just learned, he noticed that the Adjutant General School was not too far from Chicago, about 184 miles to the east. That would give him more time to be near Betty, Francis, and the other young ladies that his body and mind reached out for. What his choice meant regarding a future career was hazy. It was all about the moment.

His first day home, he had decided that he would see if Francis would join him for dinner at Army and Lou's, a soul-food restaurant on the South Side—75th and South Parkway to be exact. He had saved much of his salary for two months, so he felt as if he could splurge on a dinner and, perhaps, a room at Robert's Motel on 67th and South Parkway, a short cab ride from the restaurant. As it turned out, Francis could not join him for dinner, but promised to see him at some point during the time he would be at home.

His next move was to call Florence, who lived on the west side, to see if she wanted to join him for dinner. She said she was surprised to hear from him, but she agreed to go to dinner—if he would come and pick her up. He agreed and called his brother Theodore to see if he could borrow his 1955, two-door Chevy Bel Air sedan. It was a beaut— wide white wall tires, aqua color, with a white top, white trunk, and white fenders (only from the chrome on the side of the rear fenders up to the trunk). The interior also had aqua seats, of a much lighter shade.

His brother only said two words: "Be careful." Then handed him the key.

Florence lived on 14th and Flournoy, considered to be the best side of the west side. As soon as he pulled up, she stepped out of the door of the six-flat building and walked to his side of the car. When he rolled down his window, she immediately stuck her tongue down his throat and quickly stepped back to see how he would respond.

Then she said to him: "Forever cool."

They both initially just smiled at each other, eyes twinkling, and then both broke out into a hearty laugh. He got out of the car to open the door for her to get in on the passenger side, but she didn't immediately get in the car. Instead, she took his hand, pulled it around her waist, laid her body against his, wrapped both arms around him, and just held him for a moment. That was Florence—always up for a surprise, a warm and gentle embrace, and a lot of fun.

When she finally got in the car, she told him: "I know of a nice French restaurant not too far from here. It is called Le Bastille. Would you like to try that out?"

He hesitated because he knew that probably meant going into downtown Chicago, still not completely amenable to the presence of Blacks. But he recalled how he and his date, Betty, on prom night had gone to the London House on Michigan Avenue and Wacker Drive. They saw Stan Kenton that evening, and he still had the picture of himself posing with several other fellows. When the picture was taken, there were only four fellows and no ladies at the table. He never knew where the ladies were when the picture was taken, but he liked the pose he had struck: he was turned slightly to the right, head down a bit, and right hand across his chest but not on it. Forever cool.

He turned to Florence and said: "Sounds good. I've never eaten in a French restaurant, but I think I'd like to try it."

She gently put her hand on his knee, smiled, and said, "I knew you would!"

Playfully, he reached for the gear and acted as if his hand had accidentally slipped off the gear onto her thigh.

She giggled and said, "Watch it, buddy!"

He pretended to not hear her and rubbed the inside of her left thigh with his right hand.

She merely said, "I hope you know what you are doing."

He put the car in gear, and she pointed to the east to give him a start in the direction to the restaurant.

He then said to her: "I am sure if I don't know what I am doing, you will teach me."

She stuck her tongue out to moisten her lips and then replied sensuously: "Yes I will."

The trip to the restaurant was less than twenty minutes away, a trip of about eight miles. The area where the restaurant was located was a little north of the downtown area, near the Gold Coast. He got a little uneasy because this area was even less amenable to the presence of Blacks than the downtown area. She must have sensed his discomfort because she reached out and held the top of his right hand, still on the steering wheel, with just the right touch—his lack of ease dissipated just as easy as it appeared.

As they pulled up to the restaurant, he thought to himself: '*Looks pretty ordinary to me.*' But he knew Florence—not much was ordinary about her regarding character, looks, or actions. He got out of the car and went to the passenger side to help her alight from her carriage: Queen of Queens. She was wearing old style stockings with a garter belt to hold them up, and a little skin could be seen between the top of the stockings and the apparatus that held the garter.

He thought to himself: '*God, that's sexy. I wonder why all women don't still wear stockings and garter belts.*' He held his breath, held out his hand for her to take, and gently helped her out of the car. She did that other thing, too, as she came out of the car. She took his hand, pulled it around her waist, laid her body against his, wrapped both arms around him, and just held him for a moment—this time, she added a kiss in the mouth—not long; just a tease.

As they approached the restaurant, he observed that it was on the second floor of an old building on Oak Street just west of Rush Street. To get in, you had to go upstairs in the back of the building. There was not a front entrance, but there were several fire escapes leading from windows on each side of the rear stairway. The maitre d' greeted them in French and showed them to a table in a section of the restaurant with very subdued lighting.

He asked her: "Does the maitre d' know you? He called you by your full name."

She replied: "Yes."

His stomach churned a little. He wasn't sure if he wanted to know any more or how he might pursue the conversation, but he was one who always thought he could deal better with the known than the unknown.

So he said, "You have been here before?"

She replied, "Yes, several times."

His stomach was in a knot now. But he had gotten out there now. She went on to tell him that her apartment and car were paid for by a rich, married White man who occasionally came to visit her. In two years time, they had only been intimate three times, but he came and spent the night with her once a month—and most of the time they only ate and talked.

Florence continued to detail for Justin how she and her friend had gone to the Blue Note, London House, and several other jazz venues in the downtown area called the Loop and other nearby areas. They had also been to Le Bastille for dinner several times. But that was the limit of their being out in public. He was very prominent and not inclined to be out in public with a Black woman—or any woman for that matter, except his wife.

He moved his body away from her. Under the table, she grabbed his chair and pulled him closer to her. He tried to move back, but before he could move, she had already started to fondle him under the table and inside of his pants, and she looked him in the eyes seemingly to dare him to move.

He tried to recall how they had met and how they had become such good friends. They had dated, but they had not been intimate. When the first convulsions struck him, he tore his body away from her and realized that he was now sitting several feet away from her. He did not know what the fuck that was about. Initially embarrassed, he then saw that the action at his table was going on all around him with equal or more intensity.

She beckoned him to come back to the spot he had been in, and immediately stuck her tongue down his throat. She tried again to fondle him by putting her hand inside of his pants. This time, he asked her to use a napkin so that he could look decent when they left the restaurant.

Just as they started up again, the waiter came over to take their order for dinner.

When they left the restaurant, he was silent. It wasn't that he hadn't enjoyed the evening. He had. All of it. It was more of a contemplative mood with him trying to figure out this person he was now with. Before the moments in the restaurant, he had thought of Florence as an attractive, lively, and unassuming young lady—ready for a good time, a good hug, and a good conversation. Now he could think of only one word: seductress.

He did not know what the word seductress meant in all of its nuances, but he was sure it captured Florence, as much as a single word can capture any human being. He smiled at that thought and turned to her and saw her with a defiant look on her face that he thought said: "I dare you to judge me."

He took her hand and said: "Take me home with you tonight. I want to be with you—not just for sex. I want to embrace you as a woman and learn your secrets. I want to understand how you go out in the world and make the choices you make."

She smiled and then laughed so hard that tears rolled down her face, and she choked a bit. She then replied: "Sorry. You were really serious when you said that."

He felt embarrassed and felt she was making fun of him.

She continued: "Why don't we take this in stages. Let's just fuck tonight and see where that takes us. I am sure you are all right with that. Right?"

He nodded and put the car in gear. The ride home was in silence, verbally, but they rubbed each other in a gentle way that expressed more than lust. He felt that each wanted to touch the other's spirit or soul and immerse in that dimension of the other person. In spite of her making fun of him, he knew that she had understood what he was asking for.

He felt she knew, in spite of his silence, that he understood that she needed more time to process what he was saying. She told him that she might be up for more than physical intimacy, but starting there would give her more time and distance to think about what he had said. She also told him that her White gentleman friend liked talking, but he always talked about himself and his world. Justin wanted her to talk about herself and her world.

He had always thought that in every relationship between a man and a woman (and perhaps all relationships), there is a price that each person has to pay for being in that relationship. Everybody, at some level, understands this. The problem becomes one of not knowing what the price will be. As a rule, the price is always one that is much greater than either what one expected to pay or is able to pay. That is when the relationship becomes problematic. He wondered what would be the price for this relationship with Florence. And what would be the price she would have to pay for this relationship with him. In that instance, they were in front of her building.

When they entered her apartment on the third floor of her building, she turned to him and grabbed him with both hands to pull him up close to her firm, pointy breasts.

She said: "I don't want to fuck. I want to talk."

He nodded his head a little and took her to a couch near a window facing the front of the apartment.

"You've made some assumptions," she said. "First, that I have some secrets—at least ones that I want to reveal and can articulate. Second, you assume that when I am out in the world making choices that I have some rational and reasonable basis that I myself understand. Third, you assume that I am bright enough to engage in this conversation. Lastly, that if we started this conversation you want to have that I would be sufficiently interested enough to stay engaged long enough to satisfy you—and me. Think about that while I get some champagne for us."

With that, she rose and walked into the kitchen to get champagne glasses and a bottle of Moet-Chandon champagne from the refrigerator.

Although he meant to say the word "like"; when she returned, he said: "I really love you, girl!"

She slightly cocked her head to the right side in response to the words, and repeated one word as if it were a question:

"Love?"

He surprised himself and said, "Yes, love." They sat mostly in silence and sipped champagne for about an hour.

She then just said, "Come on."

She took his hand and led him into her bedroom—immaculate and nicely decorated by any standard. It was in that setting that he (and perhaps her, he thought) would have a standard for intimacy set for them that would endure for a long time; and, in some ways, that carried regret.

When he awoke that next morning, she was gone to work. She left a note and a key to her apartment on the nightstand. The note said, "I had to go to work. I did not want to disturb you. You looked so peaceful and angelic sleeping! Breakfast is on the stove—just heat and eat (smile). I know you have to see other people while you are home, but I would like to see you before you leave for Indianapolis. When you come by, just use the key to let yourself in. Call before you stop by (smile)."

Curious about what she had left him for breakfast, he went to the kitchen and saw a plate with a pile of grits with butter already in it, two eggs over easy, two biscuits, two slices of bacon—crispy, and two link sausages—well done all over. He fell in love again.

As he dressed, washed up, and ate the food that she had prepared; he wondered why he had been so comfortable in her bed and arms. He knew much of his comfort had to do with her beauty, intellect, and seductive ways. That made sense intellectually, but somehow that did not adequately capture how he felt. As he drove the car back to his brother, he was still thinking about Florence.

When they had started out last evening, he had only wanted companionship for the evening—nothing more. Somehow it ended up being one of those glorious moments in life that made him happy—no, ecstatic—whenever he thought about it. He came to realize, this was also one of those moments in life that sometimes made him blue because he could not hold on to the moment and make it last forever. He was sure that that was what having the blues was mostly about.

To distract himself from thinking about Florence, he turned on the radio. "Love is Strange" by Mickey and Sylvia was playing on the radio. He loved the riff on the guitar and smiled when he heard it. He also chuckled at the words "once you get it, you'll never wanna quit."

In his circles, they not only would Bop but also Cha-Cha to this tune. He had really settled into a happy place as the song ended. He hadn't stopped thinking about Florence, but he felt good—until the next song started to play. Sam Cooke's "You Send Me" came on, and he began to cry. He had no idea why he was crying, but he decided to let it flow.

He stopped and bought gas for the car, then headed to his brother's house. Theodore wasn't home, so he left the car keys with his brother's lady friend and told her where the car was parked. He grabbed a cab and headed farther south to where his mother and youngest brother now lived.

He rang the doorbell, and when his mother opened the door, the first words out of her mouth were, "How can you come to town and not first check in here?"

His mother had apparently heard from one of his brothers that he was in town.

He replied, "I honestly don't know, mom."

She had always pegged him as the "lost son," so she accepted his answer because of that and because she thought it was a genuine response. His mother offered breakfast, but he declined and decided instead to go back to sleep. In spite of the prior evening, it was comforting to be in his own bed in his own house.

CHAPTER FIVE

Love and Peace

When he got up that afternoon, he tried to reach Francis, but her mother told him that she had decided to go to Spellman College early, although her classes would not start until January. Her mother added: "Her boyfriend decided to drive her to Atlanta and spend a few weeks with her before classes started."

That was a huge disappointment, but he already understood that her head, if not her heart, was somewhere else. He turned to the southeast and blew her a kiss. That ending was in the cards; so he knew he did not have a right to anything but fond memories and positive thoughts of her.

He decided to go back to Florence's house, but he knew that was not possible until he had spoken to her. As he sat near the phone in his mother's house, he realized that he had not contacted Betty, but he had talked to two other women and spent the night with one. He picked up the phone and dialed Betty's number. Her auntie answered the phone and told him that she had not gotten in from school and work and that she would tell her that he had called.

A few hours later, Betty called him back. She was clearly not in a good mood, and she told him that. He asked why, and she told him that she had heard that he had been in town since early yesterday.

She asked, "Why did you not call me yesterday when you got in?"

He replied, "I just did not think about calling you."

He knew that she knew why he had not thought about calling her, and he also knew why she decided not to push the matter.

She immediately went to, "Will I see you tonight?"

He told her he was not sure, but he would let her know later. The truth of the matter was that he found himself vacillating on his earlier decision to see Florence that day. He tried to sort through his indecisiveness, and he could attribute part of his indecisiveness to the recent call from Betty. Given the events of the last evening, he wondered how he could even entertain the thought of not seeing Florence again before he left. But as soon as that flashed through his mind, he recognized that last evening was precisely why he was vacillating about going back to see Florence.

He remembered that he only had a week left in the city, and then he would be gone for almost three months and after that perhaps as long as two and a half years. The thought of being away from Betty that long was somewhat comforting. The thought of being away from Florence that long was unsettling. He was afraid of her propensity to be a seductress and what that might mean for a future relationship if any relationship at all. He even tried to envision being married to either Betty or Florence. Neither scenario made him happy, but he could see himself at least comfortable with Betty.

Instead of going to see either Betty or Florence, he called his youngest brother to see if he wanted to hang out with him that evening. It was early November and the second part of Indian summer in Chicago had arrived. In Chicago, Indian summer was absolutely marvelous. He could still feel the warmth and humidity off the Gulf of Mexico; and because it was Indian summer, it was somehow different from the usual and other warm and hot days of summer.

He had always felt that Indian summer in Chicago enveloped the city in a way that made him feel like he was in the Caribbean, and enveloped his body as if he was in paradise. He thought: '*Just as Chicago's winters could chill to the bone and make you want to run for cover; Chicago's Indian summers could warm to the bone and make you think about love— and sometimes sex when the wind would move the skirts of the ladies high enough to see a flash of the thigh.*'

He again borrowed his older brother's car, and with his youngest brother at his side, he set off to barhop for the evening. He and his youngest brother liked each other a lot—mostly because they shared similar interests—music, dancing, books, and pretty women! He felt good as they drove north to visit a few places on 47th Street.

He thought to himself: '*It's great to be here with my brother as a companion, free from all of the high expectations of spending a lot of money, being charming and witty, drinking more than you want to, getting caught up in someone else's bullshit notions of the world, and fucking beyond a point that allows that endeavor to be exciting and fulfilling.*'

That was what made Florence special—she did not mind spending her money or just spending an afternoon sitting and drinking champagne—no conversation required. And when she decided to make love to him, it went beyond just two bodies being in motion in some defined space. It was as if spirits and bodies were fused and transported to some intime corner of the universe.

His brother, who loved to sing, touched him on the arm to get his attention about a tune that had started to play on the radio and that he had started to hum and then sing full force. Sam Cooke's tune, "You Send Me," was playing again. At first, he was a little melancholy, but he jumped into the moment and tried to harmonize with his brother, a much better singer. In spite of that, at times, he could hear a rather pleasant bit of sound emanate from the two of them. They loved doing that and slapped hands when the song was over.

The first stop was the Peps, where they knew they would find good music, dancing, and lots of pretty young women. He had heard that the Peps was formerly known as Warwick Hall and a place for many young musicians, such as Nat "King" Cole and Louis Armstrong, to practice their craft in the late 20's and early 30's.

He had learned from experience that the Peps was now one of those places where various strata of the Black community would assemble to Bop, Walk, and slow dance. The age skew was towards the young people in the community, but the socioeconomic distribution was all over the place. At the Peps, he knew he could find a wide variety of young people—from the nouveau riche to those who were "dirt poor," as his grandmother use to say.

The Peps was on the second level of a building east of South Parkway Avenue, and he had to climb a narrow set of stairs (more than thirty in number) to get to the entrance. Each time he climbed the stairs to enter the hall, he always wondered what would happen if some catastrophic event occurred and a lot of people had to get down those stairs and out.

He always assumed that another exit existed, but he never saw it. The hall itself was just one big open space with a hardwood floor that

31

was shinier than any he had ever seen. Of course, that kind of surface made it easy to move on, so most people on the dance floor always looked as if they were gliding.

As the two of them stepped into the hall, his stomach did a little flip-flop. To his left stood Francis talking with a tall fellow that he assumed was her boyfriend and the high school basketball star that he had heard of but never seen. And across the room, straight ahead, was Betty slow dancing with a fellow who had her wrapped up like a fur coat on a woman walking down Michigan Avenue on a sub-zero day in Chicago. Before he could think about what to do, Francis saw him and waved for him to come over.

As he approached Francis, the fellow she was with departed and left the three of them alone. She reached out and took his hand and gave him a peck on the cheek and said, "It's good to see you. How much longer are you in town?"

He in turn said, "It's good to see you, too. I have about a week left before I have to head off to Indianapolis for advanced training." Then he introduced his brother, Calvin.

Before he could ask about the information he had been given by her mother, she offered: "We started driving to Atlanta yesterday; but about half way there, we decided we would stay here in Chicago for a few more weeks and go to Atlanta after New Year's Day."

He heard the words but in that instant he could only stare at her gorgeous face and long for a bit of privacy so that they could have sex and talk. He had not noticed that her boyfriend was back with them with two drinks in hand and a curious look on his face. By that time, Betty had also joined them, initially unnoticed. This time, he took the lead and introduced himself, his brother, and Betty to Francis and her boyfriend, Carl, who seemed relieved to see Betty with him and his brother.

Carl suggested that they all sit at the same table, and Francis appeared surprised by that suggestion. About five or six dances into the evening, his brother had snared a young lady who appeared eager to join him and the others at the table. She was a cutie, in a lot of different ways—full-figured, articulate, charming, and an effervescent smile. His brother had always had a taste for plenitudinous women.

When The Penguins' "Earth Angel" came on, he asked Betty to dance with him. She hesitated, and he thought it might be because she knew that the conversation would eventually turn to her being there in the arms of another fellow. But he decided to play it off and not talk about it. After all, Francis was there, and he was as much upset by her being with another man as he was upset with Betty being held so close by a dude he had seen before in the neighborhood.

As they walked to the dance floor, Betty leaned over and softly whispered in his ear: "I love you. Please marry me."

He did not verbally respond just then, but he did squeeze her hand tighter as they moved to the dance floor. He pulled her up close and said: "Yes," allowing for any interpretation of that one word that Betty wanted to give it. He did add, "You are my earth angel"—at which they both guffawed.

That instance allowed them not to worry about the future or the past. And they surrendered to the low lights, music, and movement of their bodies together. It was a lovely respite from the tension they had borne earlier in the evening, and they both just let it carry them to a more felicitous place.

As the music ended and they returned to the table, he noticed that Francis had a dour look on her face that approached being menacing. She continued to glare at him and Betty even after they were again seated. Betty did not help with the situation because she continued to hold his hand and tilted her body towards his. It was obvious that whatever went down on the dance floor was something that Betty wanted to hold on to—even for a short while. He suspected, too, that she was able to sense that he and Francis had some significant relationship even if she could not discern what it was.

Carl precipitately grabbed Francis' hand and seemed to drag her to the dance floor. He could tell that they were having an argument, but he also knew she would overwhelm him with her volume, emotionality, thought processes, and body movements; which at one point went from frantic and jerky to calm and sensuous.

Shortly after that, Carl appeared to have succumbed, and he placed both hands around Francis' waist and fell silent. As they danced, Francis looked over Carl's shoulder at him and sneered. He winced and reached for Betty's hand to console himself. He could not reconcile that moment in time with all of the others that had preceded it in relationship to her, so he just spaced-out. A few minutes later he got up and went to the restroom.

When he returned to the gathering at the table, he hit his brother on the shoulder and said, "Let's go."

His brother looked up at him and pointed to the young lady that had joined them.

He politely said, "Bring her."

He then bowed to those still at the table and took his leave. Once he hit the bottom step of the stairwell exiting the hall and stepped into the street, he took a deep breath and exhaled. The evening was still warm and delicious, filled with the poignancy of lost love, lost innocence, and lost memories. He decided to drop his brother and the young lady off at his mother's house. The young lady lived just a short distance from there on Stewart Avenue. He knew they would be safe.

He called Florence, but she did not answer. He also called his brother Theodore, but he did not answer, either. He decided to give his brother cab fare, and he headed to the lakefront with a pint of Manischewitz wine in his pocket. He had to pass Juliet's house to get to the lakefront; and on a lark, he just turned down Prairie Avenue and stopped in front of her house.

He sat for a while in front of the house, but finally got out and walked up and rang her doorbell. He started to leave at the same time that Juliet pulled back the curtain covering the glass in the front door and clicked the lock to let him in. They both expressed surprise at seeing each other, and they embraced and kissed like friends who had not seen one another for years. He and Juliet sat on the stoop in front of her house and drank the cheap, warm wine like winos from the neighborhoods they both knew well.

It had not been years since they last saw each other, but it had been more than a year since they had graduated from high school. So they spent a little time talking about where their classmates were or what they were doing. One couple had married and moved lock, stock, and barrel to Minnesota. Another had married and divorced within the same period of time. Many had gone off to college right after graduation. Still others had gotten jobs and were working downtown or in factories on the far South Side. And a few, like him, had joined various branches of the Armed Forces. When he told her he had joined the Army and was headed to Indianapolis in a few days, she turned her head away from him and dropped her head a bit.

When he stood up, his intent was to tell Juliet he was leaving and going to the lakefront, but instead, he invited her to go to the lakefront with him. She agreed and went into the house to tell her parents where she would be. As they drove east to the lakefront, she took his right arm and placed it around her shoulder and moved her body up under him. He only smiled. He had never known her as someone who liked to snuggle. But she was comfortable, and he wanted very much to give her comfort—in part because he had missed her so much and had not realized it until now. He smiled when he thought about what she had written in his graduation yearbook: '*To the boy who never gave me a chance. I wish the best of luck. May you be the top in everything you do. Love and Kisses, Juliet.*'

The lakefront was only a short distance from Juliet's house, and they could have walked there, but he chose to drive there because it allowed them other options in terms of a place to be. The lakefront on 39th Street was indeed crowded, so they opted to just take a ride down Lake Shore Drive, eighteen marvelous miles of parks and beaches that bump right up against the southwest tip and shoreline of Lake Michigan. It was mostly this part of Chicago that made him always think that Chicago was the only place to be in the summer.

As he reached the northern end of Lake Shore Drive, he turned his head slightly and saw Juliet looking at him sardonically.

She then said, "Why did you come to my house this evening?"

He could only reply, "I am not sure. It was done on an impulse. Why do you ask?"

She sarcastically replied, "None of your other women would have sex with you?"

He hesitated for a moment and then said, "I did not want to have sex with any of my other women, as you put it. You came to my mind as I drove away from the Peps, so I turned right instead of left and stopped by your house. I am glad I did. I hadn't realized how much I missed you; how much I loved you—even at a distance. You were my first real love, and that is how I will always remember you. As I said, I have joined the Army, and I am headed to Indianapolis in a few days. Stopping by to see you is one of those events that you are glad that happened, but you never really know why it happened."

She looked at him and said, "It really does not matter. Just take me to Robert's Motel and spend the rest of the evening holding me—and whatever else we may be inclined to submit to."

Tears started to roll down her cheek, and she softly laid her head on his shoulder and tried desperately not to break down totally and bawl. Her expressed emotions at points were alternately a quiet sob and a body-shaking, convulsive blubber. That aroused him in a manner that surprised him. It must have aroused her, too. She opened his shirt and started to rub his chest and play with his nipples.

By the time they were in the motel room and making love, only death would have prevented them from reaching an orgasm—together. That is what they had always done—waited on each other to reach a climax. Hers were always noisy and physical, followed by crying and a deep sleep—often with snoring.

Over the years, he would come to categorize women according to how they acted as they embraced their orgastic state. Most women, he thought, were like Juliet, but many others were on a continuum on both sides of her primordial screams—screams that connected them all to the center of life and the universe.

To the extreme left of Juliet on the continuum are the "howlers"— literally. He always thought this orgasmic expression was probably the one left over from early man and maybe even other primates who preceded primitive man. To the extreme right of Juliet are the "quiet ones." In contrast to the howlers, the quiet ones offer only a quiet sound that almost sounds like a baby who is just starting to cry: Ehh, Ehh, Ehh. He often wondered which of the extremes had the deepest orgasm. The howlers appeared to have the longest.

Neither he nor Juliet wanted to stop the flow of the evening. He told Juliet to rest on top of him, and they went to sleep in that position for several hours. He woke up when he felt Juliet lift her body off of his. Although she was smiling, he wasn't sure what her mood was.

So he said, "You ok?"

She said, "Yes. Why do you ask?"

He replied, "I just have a feeling that you are in a place that's both good and bad, and I wondered what that might bode for the future."

She stared into his eyes for a while and said: "Very perceptive. But you always were like that. I am sad because I know that you are leaving and that I might not see you again—and certainly not as a lover. I am happy that you came to see me and that we made love. About that I am also just a little sad. What I am most happy about is that I had another chance to connect with you and revisit those feelings I had when I first saw you and when we first danced at my house five years ago. As for what all of this evening means for the future—mine and yours—I don't have a clue."

With that, she took both of his hands into her hands and held them to her lips for a few seconds and then placed each of his hands on each of her still-bare breasts. She then got up and dressed. He followed suit and got dressed, too.

He held her hand as he drove her back to her house, and he continued to hold her hand as he walked with her to the entrance of her home. They had not spoken to one another since leaving the motel. When they hit the top step of the porch to her home, they both just let each other's hand go. He stood and watched her unlock the door to her house, open the door to enter, and close the door without ever saying another word or looking at him.

He turned around, walked back to the car, got in the seat, and sat for a few minutes thinking about Juliet and the evening they had together. He seldom thought of Juliet after that, and he wound up marrying Betty, his first wife.

CHAPTER SIX

Love and Separation

Just as he had feared, as soon as he had finished his training at the Adjutant General School in Indianapolis, Indiana; he had been shipped overseas to an Army installation called Neureut Kaserne in Karlsruhe, Germany—a small town in southwest Germany on the French-German border and the Rhone-Rhine River.

For the first few days in Germany, he was melancholy and somewhat afraid because of the thoughts he had harbored about Germany before he had even joined the Army. So he went to work every morning as a military stenographer (actually a secretary for the commander of the post), and never thought much about anything else except the lovely women he had left behind in Chicago. And then things got a little bit better.

He met several dudes from the south and west sides of Chicago: Two brothers, Adrian and Jim Peterson, from the west side; Joe Gamble, Frank Conner, and Mark Freeman from the south side. All of them worked in the two battalions that made up the 516th Signal Group, which provided communication support for CENTAG (Central Army Group) and, at some point, became part of the NATO defense forces in Germany after World War II.

He remained on the post and in the barracks for almost three weeks after arriving in Germany, and he only occasionally went to the PX (post exchange) and enlisted men's service club. At the service club, he started to cultivate friendships, and would often sit with the guys from Chicago and talk about what was happening back home. During the early evening hours one weekday evening, one of the Peterson brothers,

Jim, extended an invitation to him to join a group of fellows who were going to meet at the service club and take a cab into town to visit one of the local beer halls. He reluctantly accepted the invitation.

As the group gathered that Friday afternoon in the service club at Neureut Kaserne, he recognized that he was no longer afraid of being off post in Germany, and he surmised that that had to do with the fact that he had companions from Chicago at his side. As the five of them piled into one of the cabs lined up outside the post, he made an inquiry about Adrian Peterson, who was not with the group. His brother, Jim, said he had "pulled" guard duty for the evening.

Jim then said to him, "You don't have to do guard duty, do you?"

He was startled by the question because he had not thought of being or not being on guard duty. He had had guard duty at Fort Carson, so he knew exactly what it meant to be on guard duty, especially in the cool, evening, high altitude areas at the foot of Cheyenne Mountain in Colorado. Not having guard duty in Germany was one of the privileges of being assigned to headquarters of the 516th.

His reply to Jim Peterson was one word, "No."

Jim smiled and then said, "I wish I had it like that, brother."

The ride to the Gasthaus (beer hall) took only about ten minutes, but it was through the small village of Neureut with its small, continuously winding roads and near-accidents. When the cab stopped, and everyone got out, Jim Peterson stuck out his hand to collect a few deutsche marks from each fellow to pay the cab driver. He then led the way into the place as if he were a big shot. The owner of the beer hall greeted Jim with a vigorous handshake and an embrace. Jim spoke to him in German, and he obliged Jim by responding to him in English.

As best as he could make out, their leader told the owner that he had brought a new friend from the Kaserne to have a few beers and to introduce him to the locals and the world outside of the Army installation. He added, after a brief pause, that the new soldier with him was a friend who was also from his hometown of Chicago, and then he pointed to him. The owner looked in his direction and then beckoned to one of the waitresses by raising his hand and calling out, "Fraulein." An attractive, statuesque woman approached the group and took them to a table on the other side of the room. As they sat down, the jukebox not far from them started up, and Doris Day began to sing a song he had not heard before: "A Very Precious Love."

By the time the waitress brought the dark brown bottles of beer and drinking mugs to the table, he had already started to cry. The other guys at the table just smiled. They understood what he was about in that moment. So they just let his tears flow, and they drank their beers and talked softly. When the song ended, Jim raised his hands and signaled to the Fraulein to bring another round of beer to the table. When she had finished serving the beer, Jim took her hand and pulled her down to him and whispered something in her ear in German. She smiled and nodded her head before leaving.

About fifteen minutes later, the waitress came back to the table, leaned over to whisper in Jim's ear, and slid a piece of paper on the table towards him. Jim took the paper, folded it, and stuck it in the left pocket of his Eisenhower jacket, which they all wore that evening. Shortly after the waitress left the table, Jim got up and signaled him to come to the men's room.

In the men's room, Jim said to him: "There is no hurry for you to do this, but here is the name, telephone number, and address of a Fraulein who lives nearby. For this evening, we have already told her you were coming, but we will confirm that with her if you actually want to go tonight. She is a good friend of the waitress. She is not a prostitute, but you will have to give her money to be with her. That is just her way of surviving. She is clean, so you don't even need to wear a rubber. Oh, the one problem is that she lives off-limits. So when you get to her street, you will have to run a few feet down an alley to get to her place. Usually, there are no MPs around. But be careful."

He hadn't brought much money with him, so he said to Jim: "I need about forty dollars. I will give it back to you when we get back to the base. Are you guys going to wait for me?"

Jim hesitated and then just replied, "Yes."

Jim then walked with him to the door, pointed to the east, and said, "Turn right and go about a half block. You will see an off-limits notice on both sides of a wall at the alley and the sidewalk entrance to the alley. That is where you will go. The Fraulein will be called, and she will meet you outside of her place."

With that, Jim pushed him out of the door of the Gasthaus. Jim must have recognized his hesitation to move down the street. But after he was out of the door, he ran the half-block to the corner, made a right turn, ran about twenty-five feet to the signs that said off-limits, and then, after he hesitated for a moment, made another right turn down the dimly lit alley. At the end of the alley, he saw a woman who beckoned him to come over to her.

He entered the rather small apartment that had most of the windows covered with dark drapes. He could barely see the woman's face because of the small amount of light in the room. When she moved into the light that was available in the room, he saw that she was a woman in her late forties or early fifties. Her face had started to wrinkle and sag, but you could tell that she had once been a very attractive woman. She spoke broken English, and he spoke only a little German; but they managed to communicate that he would have to pay forty Deutsche Marks (around ten dollars) for her services.

As they both undressed, he became a little uncomfortable, and the look on her faced suggested the she sensed his discomfort. She told him to relax, and after fifteen minutes, the whole event was over. He hurriedly dressed, gave her the money, and reversed his route to the Gasthaus. As he ran from the restricted area, he had already decided that he would not do that again.

It was not at all satisfying, although he did feel some physical relief of tension in his body. What he got in that moment did not go much beyond masturbation. Before that night, he had always been involved with women at a level of sexual intimacy that moved him deeply. Contrary to popular thought and belief, his always got better after the first time.

Most of his buddies at the Gasthaus were now dancing and drinking with several young ladies; some of them appeared to be underage. They were surprised to see him back so soon because they assumed he would spend the night with the Fraulein. He had not entertained that as an idea until his buddies talked about it.

He sat quietly at the table with his keg of beer and thought about what had just happened. He then panicked. '*Should he have used protection?*' Just as that thought popped into his mind, "Love is Strange" by Mickey and Sylvia started to play on the jukebox. His shoulders dropped a little, and a wry smile came across his face. He thought to himself: '*I have more than two more years to be here. Is this it?*'

CHAPTER SEVEN

Love Nearby

In spite of entreaties from his buddies from Chicago, he did not venture off the post for three months after that little jaunt to the Gasthaus and his little side trip from there. What he did do was to spend a lot more time in the enlisted men's service club. His initial interest there was a Black woman who worked in the club as a hostess. She was one of six hostesses that staffed the enlisted men's service club, and when she walked, she made all the right moves. Her name was Lynne, and when he first tried to talk to her, she wouldn't give him the time of day, as the old folks use to say. He persisted, but she was resolute in her efforts not to give him any play.

Then one evening he noticed that one of the other hostesses at the club was staring at him and smiling, kind of a demure smile. She finally decided to come over to him and have a conversation. Her name was Eileen, and she was White. Eileen was very attractive—almost flawless except for a front tooth that bumped too much up against another front tooth. Eileen's legs were big and nicely shaped. She had a nice little bump for a butt, but not as inviting as Lynne. She was tall for a woman, and her small waist and ample (but not huge) bust gave her a classic, hourglass figure. He had talked with her many times before, but this conversation had a decidedly different feel. There was something different about Eileen this particular evening. He wasn't sure what was different, but he decided to play it as it lay.

Eileen offered up information on a jazz concert (and an invitation to join her) that was coming to Heidelberg, located about thirty miles

northeast of Karlsruhe, the largest German city near the small town of Neureut.

At first, he had said no, but then she said: "This is a jazz concert featuring Art Blakey and the Jazz Messengers. Are you sure you want to miss this? My treat."

He thought to himself, '*Oh, shit!*'

He quickly said, "Ok. Tell me more about a time and how we can get there."

As she continued, the offer got better. She added, "Lee Morgan is now playing with the Messengers, along with Benny Golson and Bobby Timmons. This has to be one of the best jazz groups around today. The concert starts at 7:00 P.M., and we can leave about 5:30. It is only about a half-hour drive from here."

She then laughed and said, "On the autobahn, it will probably take fifteen minutes."

He stared into her eyes, and she stared back. His stomach got tight as he thought to himself: '*Who is this bitch that knows as much as I do, and maybe more, about jazz.*'

Since joining the Army, he had not kept up with the Jazz Messengers or jazz in general, for that matter. He thought Horace Silver was still the pianist for the group. She had hooked him. He liked having a woman to share his interest in jazz.

Since she was working at the club that evening, she abruptly got up and said: "See you here in front of the club on Saturday at 5:30 P.M."

As she walked away to talk with other dudes in the club, he watched her gorgeous legs move inside of a skirt that was tight at a helm that was just a little above the knees. The skirt itself was not real tight, but it was tight enough to accentuate her cute behind and lovely waist. He only smiled and walked over to the pool table where one soldier was waiting for another person to shoot pool with him.

She was smoking an American filtered cigarette of some kind (Marlboro or Winston) and sitting in a convertible Austin Healey when he walked up to the service club. He could only smile and shake his head a little. The car's color was primrose yellow over black, and shiny like it was right out of the dealership. She got out of the driver's seat, went to the passenger's side, and stood to wait for him to open the door for her to get in.

He took no offense at that gesture because he thought that was the way all men and women conducted themselves under the circumstances. He opened the door and took one of her hands so she could easily slide down into the seat. He walked around to the driver's side, got in, and said: "You are sure you want me to drive?"

She never turned her face to him, but calmly said: "Yes, I want you to drive, and I know that you can drive a stick-shift vehicle because I see you sometimes driving Colonel Mackey's staff car."

He put the car in gear, drove to the entrance of the Kaserne, and turned right, just the opposite of the direction to the town of Neureut. He was a little rusty at first because the colonel's staff car had the gearshift in the steering column instead of in the floor of the car. As he headed to the autobahn, she shifted in her seat to get more comfortable. She then placed her left hand on his right knee even though she knew he would have to move his knee often to shift gears. He did not object to her hand being there, and thought to himself: '*If we hit a bump or there is sudden motion in the car, this ought to be fun.*'

He thought the drive on the autobahn to Heidelberg was probably one on the loveliest in the world. You have to go through a region bounded on the east by the Neckar River and on the west by the Rhine River. Part of this region has an area called the Black Forest that they could see in the distance. With that view of the Black Forest, the warm summer breeze, the top dropped on the convertible, and her hand on his knee; he could only breathe spasmodically and melt into the moment. Heaven redefined.

It only took them a little more than eighteen minutes to reach Heidelberg. They flew past Tubingen, Stuttgart, and Heilbronn in no time at all. As they exited the autobahn to the town of Heidelberg, he got a panic attack from out of nowhere, and he pulled over to the shoulder of the autobahn to rest a moment. She got out of the car, came to his side of the car, and gave him mouth-to-mouth resuscitation of some sort.

Jokingly, she said: "I got it from here, soldier. Let me show you how to really drive a stick."

With that, she had him get in the passenger's seat, and she got in the driver's seat.

She asked him, "Can I kiss you?"

He said, "Yes." Then he turned to kiss her on the mouth.

She said, "No, I mean can I really kiss you!"

Before he could respond, however, she had already unzipped his pants and started to fondle him first with her hands and then her lips. That only lasted a hot minute.

He sheepishly said, "Now what."

She wryly smiled and said: "Nothing."

He was not sure what she meant, but it had both a foreboding and delectable meaning at the same time. As she put the car in first gear, his body involuntarily shook for the last time, and he nodded off several times for a second or two.

The concert was at the Karlstorbahnhof, an old train station that had been converted into a venue for events of various kinds. The hall was packed. There were a lot of young people in the crowd, mostly Germans; but the majority of the crowd was composed of United States' servicemen from almost all of the branches. The buzz in the crowd was palpable, but he had a hard time separating his anticipation for seeing Art Blakey from his anticipation for seeing Eileen naked.

As soon as the house lights dimmed, Blakey and the Jazz Messengers jumped right into one of his favorite numbers: "Alamode," an up-tempo number featuring Lee Morgan on trumpet, with Blakey driving the group like a slave driver. Eileen was as much in the moment as he was. Out of the corner of his right eye, he watched as she clapped to the music as if she could play an instrument. She had her groove, and he had his.

The group followed "Alamode" with the tune "Invitation," whose three-quarter-time opening always made him think of elephants moving slowly through the jungle in some syncopated manner. Then came "Circus," another of his favorite jazz cuts, which featured Wayne Shorter on tenor sax and Curtis Fuller on trombone. On this number, he and Eileen were both moving their heads and body together in amazing ways. Of course, in the moment he realized how synchronized they were, he was trying to imagine them in bed making love and having mind-blowing sex.

In the next piece, "You Don't Know What Love Is," Lee Morgan took the lead, the other horns intermittently joined in, and Wayne Shorter took a beautiful solo that was followed by a positively mellow solo from Curtis Fuller. Towards the end, Bobby Timmons came in on piano so beautifully and lightly that it made him think of gossamer wings.

When the group played "I Hear a Rhapsody," he squirmed in his seat a bit. He liked hearing that tune done by vocalists, but it always struck him as too tepid when he heard it played only by jazz musicians. It just did not have the verve he associated with jazz. But he moved his legs and suffered through it. He felt the same way about the next tune played, "Gee Baby Ain't I Good to You." It was the final song before the intermission, so he sat and smiled to keep from yawning and leaping out of his seat.

The show after the intermission was even less impressive than the last two numbers before the intermission. The group returned to some tunes that had been recorded with Thelonious Monk in the late 50's. In his music library, he had a lot of songs that had been done by Monk, but none of them were being played that evening. "Evidence," was okay; on "In Walked Bud," Johnny Griffin almost pulled him in; "Blue Monk," made him think about a period in Black music that was dominated by the blues; "I Mean You," sounded familiar, but no name came to mind; "Purple Shades," another bluesy tune was a little more than he could take.

He took Eileen by the hand and gently pulled her up to follow him out even before the concert had ended. He was at a loss to understand the selections of the group for this concert, especially the second half of the show. Neither he nor Eileen said much as they left the hall.

As they walked to the car, she playfully hit him with her left hip. He smiled and gently hit her back with his right hip. That helped to end whatever funk they were in because they laughed and grabbed one another by the waist and pulled one another close and held each other tightly. They even stopped for a moment, pecked each other, and broke out laughing again. They started to talk about the concert and the tunes they most enjoyed. They both agreed that they could have left the concert at the intermission and spent that time doing some other "things."

"You want to drive back," she said.

"Yes," he replied, and stuck out his hand for the keys.

The evening was cooler, but it was still a nice drive back to the post. Before they reached the barracks, she told him to go about a mile past there to a housing development for Americans who were officers or worked as civilians for the Army.

He told her, "You know this area is off-limits for enlisted men?"

She replied, "Not if you are invited by someone who lives there."

He knew that was true because he had been to the house of an instructor who worked for the University of Maryland's Overseas Branch.

As they left the car to enter the building where Eileen lived, for the first time that evening, she took his hand and held it gently. It was an assurance of some sort, but he was already comfortable. So when they stepped out of the elevator on the fourth floor of the building, he was breathing a bit heavier than usual. Before they could even get in her apartment, he had pushed her up against the wall and raised her dress. He dropped to his knees to pull down her underwear and was surprised to find that she had none on.

He had intended to have oral sex in the hall, but she grabbed him under both armpits and pulled him up. She managed to turn the key on the lock to her apartment, and they both fell into the hall and on the floor in a fit of passion and a flurry of activities to remove clothes. Her body was nearly perfect—full breasts; wide hips; round, full buttocks. Her nipples were full and pink. Her arms and legs were nicely shaped, ready and willing.

She made love better than any woman he had known. She did not holler, scream, scratch, or kick. What she did was to stay with him: quietly, softly, gently; and then at the right moment, she submitted totally, absolutely, fully. They stayed on the floor in the hall for a while after that and whispered to each other. He told her that she was the most beautiful woman in the world, but he was just speaking of the moment when they both climaxed at the same time.

That was not the first time he became conscious of the fact that a woman is never more beautiful than in the moments she is beneath a man and coming into her orgasmic state. He had observed that for the first time when he and Francis made love for the first time. After that time with Francis, he observed that repeatedly with all of the women with whom he was intimate.

She said, "I need to tell you something."

"Ok," he said.

She did not immediately speak, but finally said: "I have a serious relationship with someone on the base. You know him well because he is in the headquarters company."

There were only about fifteen dudes in the headquarters company, so he was able to quickly flit images of each through his mind. Nothing stuck.

So he said, "Who is it?"

She hesitated again, but finally uttered the word, "Jack."

He repeated the word, "Jack?"

She said, "Yes."

He started to get up, put on his clothes, and leave. Then he realized she was holding him down on top of her with both her arms and legs.

She said, "He kind of knows about you because I have talked with him about you. When he first expressed interest in getting to know me, I told him I was interested in someone else on the base. I also told him that I had not had that interest reciprocated. He asked who it was, but I told him that I was not inclined to reveal that to him. I also told him that I would have a relationship with him concerning a future for myself, but that I would probably hold you in my heart for a long time even if we never got together."

She had him physically locked both inside of her and outside of her. He wanted to struggle to free himself but decided not to. As he lay there, he did wonder why she had decided to still be intimate with him knowing that Jack was someone who was both his colleague and friend. He wasn't Jack's drinking buddy, but they had a good relationship. Jack was the orderly for the colonel that was his boss.

He wondered how he would react when he saw Jack the next time. He shortly dozed off, and when he came to, she was still naked and sitting next to him with a cup of coffee being offered up to him. After they had sipped coffee for about fifteen minutes without speaking, she grabbed his hand and took him to her bed. This time, their lovemaking was not as frenetic, but it was just as delightful and fulfilling. Man!

He did not see Jack the next day because it was Sunday. He sauntered over to the service club to get a glimpse of Eileen. She was off he was told. He knew from that where Jack was, and he quickly left the club to go to his room. Because he was in the headquarters company, he had a private room in the NCO (non-commissioned officers) building. Out of all of the perks of being in Headquarters Company, he enjoyed this one the most. He sat down on his bunk and decided to write a letter to Betty.

A dread came over him the moment he put pen to paper. He was in a funk over the thought of Eileen and Jack being together, and only the act of writing to Betty gave him any relief. Still, he did not feel good about what that act of writing Betty might portend for him or Betty.

He had already decided when he left Eileen early that morning that he would not see her again because of her relationship with Jack, but he also understood that it would be hard to stay away from her. Her lithe body, wicked smile, subtle lovemaking, and engaging intellect all pulled him into her orbit in ways that frightened him.

He and Eileen both knew that they did not and could not have a future together. She was White and from Norfolk, Virginia, and he was Black and from Chicago. In an ideal world, those would only be superficial descriptions of people and the exact locations of places on earth. In the real world, they were trouble for both of them if they tried to be together.

He fell across his bed and closed his eyes. Images of Eileen's body flitted across his mind, and he squirmed to try to make them disappear. They would not go away, and he just surrendered to her rapture and exploded. He had barely touched himself and was just about to fall asleep when that all happened. That had never happened to him that way. He wondered where the moment would lead him, but he did not attempt to do anything except to be in the moment.

CHAPTER EIGHT

Love From Home

He woke up about an hour later, fully aware that he needed to shower and change clothes. His initial inclination was to just climb under the covers and spend the night resting. He also thought about getting a cab and returning to the beer hall where he and his Chicago buddies had gone several months earlier. As he stood in the shower fretting about Eileen again, he decided he would write to Betty and tell her that he would come home on furlough, marry her, and then bring her to Germany. She had been pushing him to do that because, as she said, "It would be a great opportunity for me to be with you and also to travel all over Europe."

A few months later, they were living in Germany in an apartment on the first floor of a building owned by a German family who lived on the second floor. He had taken a three-week furlough and flown home to Chicago. Two days after setting foot in Chicago, he was married in a lovely ceremony in the small church that he had attended since he was a small boy. The trip back to Germany with his bride in tow was a good one. He had not planned on marrying Betty that soon, but he thought that would please her and provide him with someone to love and be with in a foreign place.

In the initial months in Europe with Betty, he was extremely happy. They traveled to Munich, Stuttgart, Mannheim, Frankfurt, Bonn, and many other cities in various parts of the country. They then started to go outside of Germany: First to Paris, then to Rome, and back north to Amsterdam.

He thought his choice to bring Betty to Europe was a good one. Then one evening when he walked into their apartment, he casually picked up a letter from home that had been opened. It was from Hazel, a close friend of Betty back in Chicago. Without thinking, he read the letter just hoping to get news from home. In the letter, however, Hazel talked about this guy that Betty was having an affair with back in Chicago. The affair had started after he went to Germany and continued after he had married Betty.

That feeling that he got when he saw Juliet with the R.O.T.C. guy returned with a force that almost took him to his knees. In the letter, Hazel, who was also married, talked both about her affair with a married man and Betty's affair with a man who was single and wanted to marry her even after she had gotten married to Justin. He never mentioned to Betty or anyone else that he knew about the affair she was having back home, but it scarred him deeply.

He finished his tour of duty overseas after two more years, but he sent Betty back home a year before he left. In the interval between the time Betty returned to the States and the time he left Europe, he ran the streets of Europe like a wild beast. He became a friend of a brother out of Philly named Pat Carnigan.

Unlike him, Pat had no fear of going anywhere in Europe; and after many entreaties from Pat, he finally decided to join Pat as they went to almost every jazz concert and jazz venue in Germany, France, and the Netherlands. They saw Horace Silver, MJQ (Modern Jazz Quartet), Sonny Rollins, Miles Davis, Thelonious Monk, and most of the prominent jazz musician of the late 50's. Those times were reminiscent of what he was now experiencing: unadulterated delectation!

Shortly after he decided to travel the breadth of Europe with Pat, he was able to buy a Mercedes-Benz 170V that was said to have belonged to one of Hitler's top henchmen. He bought it for $500.00 from another soldier (a tall, thin Jewish fellow hailing from New York) who was returning to the States after two years in Germany. It was a dream car. The body was in great shape; the interior almost perfect in every way, including beige cloth seats; four-in-the-floor gear shift; an exterior that was close to a willow green; and seating for five people.

The joy of live jazz performances in some of the best concert venues in Europe and trysts with women of various "persuasions" all over Europe allowed some of the pain of Betty's infidelity to subside to a tolerable level. And that, in turn, helped him to go home to Betty and resume a fairly normal life, the pursuit of a college degree, and the search for an occupation that would support a family and satisfy his drive to create something that would give significance to his time here on earth.

He had given up his thoughts about being a chemist, something that he had pursued before his stint in the Army because of a high-school chemistry teacher, Mr. Burns. In addition to being good at conducting the experiments done in his chemistry class, he thought about chemistry as a career because Mr. Burns had convinced him that that was a good career option. After half of a semester at the University of Wisconsin, the very thought of spending his life in a science laboratory conducting experiments gave him the willies.

He and Betty found a studio apartment on 64th and Normal, and for a while things were going well. He had managed to get a good-paying job at the Post Office working the evening shift, enter Roosevelt University as a junior with history as a major, and settle down for a happily-forever-after life. Betty was in school part-time and worked full-time as an executive secretary. Life was good, but he understood that there is always pain that comes on the heels of joy.

The job at the Post Office paid well, but it did not pay consistently well. The section that he worked in was parcel post, and some weeks he got a lot of overtime because of the volume of parcel post mail. Other weeks he did not get in forty hours of work, and the postal supervisor would routinely tell everybody in his section to go home early. One day during the summer of 1961, he arrived home early to find his wife, her best friend, and the dude she had had an affair with all in bed together. Betty's only comment when he walked in was: "I needed something that you could not give me right now." He nodded his head almost imperceptibly in the direction of the threesome to acknowledge his agreement with Betty's comment. He then took off his clothes to join in the debauchery.

CHAPTER NINE

The Love of Art

He was free now. Free from any negative feelings about his wife having an affair. Free from any inhibitions about being with two women, or a man, or a man and two women! Free to give expression to whom he was sexually. Yet, he had no desire to repeat that experience. It was just taking a moment to be in a moment for a moment. Nothing more.

When he went to work the next day, he felt an incredible lightness of being. In the second that he tried to celebrate his feelings, a cute little co-worker walked past and said, "Hi." He had seen her on the floor many times, but he would only take a glance at her coming towards him, except for the one time that he looked at her from behind. He never again looked at her walking away from him. He did not even want to be tempted. However, today he was free. He did look at her from behind this time, and he was tempted. Felicia's behind was a living piece of art; but no artist could have rendered what she had more perfectly— and that was just the view in a pair of jeans.

Felicia toyed with him for several weeks by making sure that he saw her walking away from him every day, some days reversing her steps after passing by him if she thought he did not notice her. What was funny was that the instant she moved away from the conveyor belt carrying the parcel post and stepped onto the floor of the parcel post section of the Post Office to go to the washroom or to the lunchroom, someone invariably pushed the emergency button to stop the movement of boxes.

Because there was an emergency button every four or five feet along a one hundred and eighty-foot long conveyor, no one ever knew who had pushed the button. What everyone did know was that work would stop to watch Felicia walk past and Justin to pick her up like radar. Even the floor supervisors participated in this game, and some days there would be higher-ups that would come to the area just to see Felicia and Justin do a tango-like dance using only the currencies of thoughts and feelings.

When she finally took him home with her one evening, he wondered why he had been chosen, despite the fact that she had obviously been trying to get his attention for several months. There were forty guys and seven women on the floor during his shift. Forty guys and six women expressed a desire to be with Felicia in the bed, mostly just to get a better view of her behind.

Making love to Felicia was not like anything he had known—especially when they did it doggy style. He would enter her with such ease and pleasure that a more sublime version of the incredible lightness of being that he had known before would overtake and transport him to places he could neither fully describe nor fully recall.

After several years of being intimate with Felicia in a variety of places across the country, she called him one fall evening in 1967 and asked that they meet for dinner at The Flamingo restaurant in the Palmer House Hotel in the Loop. Initially just very pleased by the opportunity to eat in such a grand place, he unhesitatingly said, "Yes." Soon thereafter, however, he had reservations about his hasty answer.

His immediate thought was that this was not a special occasion, so why such a fancy and expensive place to meet. His next thought came with a lot of panic because he thought she might want to tell him she was pregnant or that she wanted to get married. He decided not to think much more about it, and just got on the State Street bus and rode downtown to State and Monroe streets.

When he entered the restaurant, located on a lower level of the hotel, he saw her sitting in a nicely lit corner of the restaurant drinking a Mai Tai and smoking a King-Size Chesterfield cigarette. She smiled at his entry to the restaurant, but it was not her usual smile. Her smile had a heaviness that he had not seen before, which prompted him to order a Black Russian instead of his usual Kahlua and cream.

She immediately noticed the change and said, "Preparing for the worst, huh?"

He tightened his lips and then said, "Yes. Let's get right to it."

She took another sip of her Mai Tai and took another drag from her cigarette before she answered.

She said, "I am engaged to be married next year in June." She then just stared at him to see what sort of response she would get.

He said to her, "Is that what you want?"

She quickly replied, "Yes."

He said to her, "Then let's order dinner and another drink; and while we wait for those to arrive, let's dance."

They both had learned to tango, so he said to the quartet leader that was playing music, "Please play something to which we can dance the tango."

After they had dinner and a few more drinks, they got a room in the hotel and spent the night talking and making love. Neither expressed regret about the time they had spent together over the years, and that morning he watched her as she went to the bathroom.

She appeared to have deliberately left the door open so that he could watch her admire her behind by looking in the bathroom mirror. His response was as visceral in the moment as it had been the first time he saw her naked from behind. Without speaking, he got up and had her bend over the sink while they made love for the last time.

CHAPTER TEN

Losing Love

He had always thought that most women wanted to be loved unconditionally, but they did not know how to love unconditionally. Felicia knew both sides of that coin, and she had helped him to begin to know how to do that. Based mostly upon that fond thought of her; in June of that following year, he traveled to Paris to participate in her wedding to a prominent jazz musician. He wanted to tell her that that would be a mistake, but he also feared that she would change her mind and want to stay in the United States and marry him, which he was not ready to do, besides already being married to Betty.

Still, he accompanied her to Paris and stood in as her bridesmaid. The ceremony was fabulous, with many jazz-musician friends in attendance: Bud Powell, Ben Webster, Freddie Hubbard, Hank Jones, Thad Jones, Gene Ammons, Kenny Clarke, and a bunch of other jazz musicians who played the European jazz scene, especially the one in Paris.

At various restaurants and at the wedding, the food was even better than he had remembered from the time when he and Betty were in Paris and still in love, a lamentation that he hoped Felicia would not be able to discern in any way in spite of her getting married. He got a cab to the Orly Airport in Paris as soon as the wedding ceremony was over. He never saw or heard from Felicia again.

When he got back to Chicago, he returned to his job of teaching. He had been assigned to the DuSable Upper-Grade Center because he was a young African-American male. At twenty-six years of age, he was one of the youngest teachers in the school system in one of the roughest schools in the city. He had left the Army with double the maturity he had had when he entered. He thought himself now prepared for whatever came his way.

As he struggled to get into the new school year, he recognized that something in his psyche had shifted. He was no longer content in some ways that he had been in the past. In the past, even in moments of profound lamentation, he had managed to maintain a certain level of joy that could also be described as happiness, a *joie de vivre*, if you will.

He did not have that *joie de vivre* after he returned from Paris, and as he stood in front of his students in his social studies class or talked with his colleagues in the teachers' lounge, his mind would wander back to encounters with Betty, Francis, Juliet, Eileen, Florence, Felicia, and a bevy of women he had known over the years but whose names and faces were now dim or altogether missing from his memory.

Part of what he recognized about his present mindset was a feeling of being stagnant. He tried to walk himself through that mentally but never got far. Another thing that he recognized about his mindset was that he was feeling financially adrift. Still, beyond both of those identifiable feelings, there was a nonspecific angst that stayed with him both in his hours awake and asleep.

To help move off of the spot he was on, he decided to return to school and get a master's in history. That helped considerably. He loved history and always thought it more fascinating than the fiction that he had read all of those years in college. He never understood why most students did not like history and associated it mostly with memorizing dates and events.

To him, history was far from being such a pedestrian notion of knowledge. At its best, it was sustained inquiry about the human condition. At its worst, it was interesting recounts of the achievements and foibles of the human race. He also got a job that summer delivering telephone books in various neighborhoods in Chicago in an effort to earn extra money.

With some satisfaction reaching deep into his spirit from his pursuit of a master's and more money in his pocket, he then found an itch for something to reach deep into his emotions. With his marriage in limbo and his libido getting stronger than ever since Felicia pushed him out her life, he caught the eye of a tall, thin, beautiful, Black woman who worked in the social studies department at his school.

Initially, they found reasons to be in each other's company related to work: chaperones or supervisors for athletics events, sponsors of student clubs, after-school work on curriculum projects or in-service activities, instructors in the GED program after regular school, and hearty participants in parties in not-too-distant clubs frequented by staff after school, especially on payday Fridays.

One evening during one of those Friday parties, she leaned over and whispered in his ear: "Come and go home with me." He gently nodded his head, and they boldly got up from the table holding hands and left the lounge on 78th and Cottage Grove. Neither of them cared that all of their colleagues knew that they were headed for the "killing floor," probably at her place since he was married. They had not ever talked about being intimate with one another, but both knew that it would happen.

She lived across the street from the school in a sparsely furnished, one-bedroom apartment. Most of the apartment was painted green, with one wall accented with purple paint. In the kitchen, there was only a small round table that sat on a pedestal and large round base that sat on a hardwood floor. On two sides of the table were two white, molded, fiberglass chairs with an all-in-one piece pedestal and large round base. The bedroom was painted the same as the rest of the apartment, but it had one accented wall in mauve. The bed in the room was king size and had a black and white comforter neatly thrown on it with a bed cover on top of it that was the same color as the green walls. Interesting!

He had expected something more vibrant or shocking, but what he saw somehow fitted her well, at least what he knew about her. She was never one to engage in a lot of conversation, but she spoke to you in ways that were very clear. Inside of the apartment that evening, she dropped her skirt on the floor, removed her blouse and bra, and kept her scanty underwear and stilettos hills on.

Her breasts and nipples were much fuller and upright than he had imagined and her hips were wider and bigger than he had hoped for. Watching him watching her, she pointed to her bedroom with a wry smile, and then she pinned him to the wall as soon as they stepped inside the bedroom. She had barely touched him before he was moaning for love. He neither remembered undressing himself nor her undressing him. But when he was again fully conscious of their seamless embrace, he almost fainted. He refocused when she said: "Don't go. Stay here with me."

Here was a woman for the ages. Her name was Scottie, which always made him think of one of the lead singers in the Whispers, an R & B group with a string of hit records, except his name was spelled Scotty. She was six feet tall, thin (but not skinny), extremely curvaceous, dark-skinned with no blemishes (she wore almost no makeup except a hint of lipstick), walked in slow-motion, danced as if she was prancing, and made love in such an elegant manner that she took your breath away with just the touch of a finger and a light kiss wherever she decided to place it.

He woke up in her bed at about 3:30 in the morning. She was sleeping and had pushed her smooth behind up against his. He rolled over, pried her legs open, and entered her from behind. They were both satisfied in just a matter of minutes, and they both drifted back to sleep for several hours.

If he had not been married, he would have taken Scottie for his wife—perhaps. This was an iffy proposition for two reasons: He was married and she was not inclined to be married. In fact, she was not even inclined to be in an exclusive, one-on-one relationship! He had heard through the grapevine that Scottie was a woman who had an affair with half of the twenty-three men in the social studies department, and she had let all of them know what she was doing. Of course that made her desired even more by all of the men in that department and in all of the other departments in the school.

After one year in the school, the sexual gravitas surrounding Scottie even spilled over into Scottie being sought after by a bunch of women in the school. Although he was never able to confirm that, it was rumored that Scottie did have trysts with many women in the school, some of whom were married.

At the end of her second year of teaching, Scottie just disappeared that summer. It was rumored that she had run off with and married a Black Militant who was also a teacher in the social studies department in the school. Reflecting on what he knew about Scottie, he doubted that that was true. As black and bright and pretty as she was, she would not have allowed herself to be confined physically or intellectually by any ideologue, no matter his persuasion, physical attributes, or talents.

He did so miss Scottie, and he spent a lot of time in the early summer trying to find her, with no success. He had no idea why finding her was important to him. What he did understand was that she was different from any woman he had known. As the old saying goes, she was in this world but not of this world. Scottie was like a spirit just spending a little time here on earth having a little fun. And you knew she was a spirit simply by the way she moved about in the world: moving in slow-motion and without effort as she walked, prancing when she danced in a way that made it appear that she never touched solid ground.

As he had observed and been told, when she stood before her classes, she never spoke above a whisper, but her students were spellbound. Her classes were the quietest and most orderly in the school. They were also the classes in the school that you knew had the most learning going on.

Another rumor had it that Scottie had moved to Kansas City, Missouri. So in the middle of that summer, he even drove there hoping to bump accidentally into her somewhere on the street or find her name listed in the phone book or available from the local telephone operator.

He also wanted to visit Kansas City because it was the original home of his favorite musician of all times: Charlie Parker. Even now, Charlie Parker was the only saxophone player he could instantly recognize by just hearing a few notes. Although Parker had died more than a decade earlier in New York, he just wanted to set foot on the hallowed grounds of Charlie Parker's birthplace in Kansas City. So he borrowed money and bought a new Mazda Cosmo and took out on Route 66 to find Scottie—whose love and lovemaking had been the sweetest, most translucent, and most ephemeral of his life.

CHAPTER ELEVEN

Finding Love

The trip to Kansas City, Missouri did not turn out the way he had hoped, but it was still a good trip. He searched high and low for Scottie, but not a trace of her could be found. One day as he stood before the grave of Charlie Parker in Blue Summit, a small hamlet just outside of Kansas City, Missouri, a woman who reminded him of Scottie approached the gravesite. She was younger and a bit shorter than Scottie, but she was beautiful and black like Scottie and even shapelier.

Initially, he tried to ignore her, but she kept looking at him and smiling. Finally, he said, "What's your name?"

She replied, "April. What is your name?"

His reply was, "Justin. Come and have lunch with me."

With that, they jumped in a cab because he had left his car at the hotel where he stayed and she had valet parked her car in the parking lot of a restaurant near where she lived and where they were now headed. They immediately held hands, smiled at each other, and moved closer so that their hips and legs touched.

Over lunch, she started to talk a little. She asked him, "Aren't you curious about how and why I sought you out at the gravesite?"

He hesitated before answering the question, but finally said: "I thought you just saw a good-looking man and decided you wanted to get to know him."

She smiled wryly, and said, "Is that the best you can do?"

He knew exactly what she was saying. He did try to come up with something better and certainly more thoughtful. But he couldn't. He was stuck on her physical presence and could not process, at any level, the moment beyond that.

He continued to look deep into her eyes, and after a few moments said: "Scottie sent you."

She smiled and replied, "There you go!"

He became a little uneasy at first but sank into his seat with a huge sigh of relief and a feeling of unbounded happiness. April told him that Scottie was her aunt and that she had returned to Kansas that summer with a disease that could be neither diagnosed nor cured. She had passed away three weeks earlier. Just minutes before passing, Scottie had told April to find him at Parker's gravesite and tell him what had happened to her. Scottie had given April the exact day and time he would be visiting Parker's grave.

He quivered then shuddered as April finished her story of how she had found him and why. He was spellbound and did not move even when the waiter brought their food to the table. He had foreseen the moment as precisely as it had unfolded on that day.

He took April's hand and said, "What is it you want of me or from me?"

She replied, "I want you to give me what you gave Scottie."

He said, "But I don't know what it is I gave Scottie."

She said, "Yes, you do. Just like you were to able to foresee me meeting you at Bird's gravesite and knowing why I was there and who sent me."

He sat silently for a few minutes, looking into her eyes to see if he could discern more about what was happening and what might happen in the future.

Before he could speak again, she gently took his right hand and held it with both of her hands and said, "Don't be afraid."

Then he heard a faint sound that appeared to be that of a small bell. He was not able to discern the direction from which it came, and he did not hear it again.

He stared at April hoping she would continue to speak and let him enjoy the food that was brought to the table. He had gumbo that contained huge shrimps, large crab legs, pieces of chicken, sausage, and large pieces of whole okra that were so delicious it was toe curling.

She had the baby-back ribs for which Kansas City was famous, and they both decided to have some of the other's food. The tension of the earlier moments dissipated as they sat and ate and talked and drank beer and champagne, which (as they learned that evening) both thought was an unusual combination since they both preferred only champagne.

She finally said, "Both Scottie and I are from Antigua. Our families came to America some years ago to find a better life and wound up here in Kansas City. We both come from a long line of strong women whose single mission is to find a man who can learn how to speak to his own soul. That is why you met Scottie, and that is why you are meeting me now."

He said to April, "But what does that mean to 'speak to his own soul'?"

She replied, "You have to be able to find meaning for and in your life, independent of what others think you should do and believe they know about you."

At a certain level, he understood precisely what she meant. At another level, he was totally baffled by her comment. Although he was sure that what he was about to ask her was not what she meant, he said: "So you mean you have to find out what your purpose in life is?"

"No, she replied. "You have to create a purpose for your life that is in keeping with what your soul needs."

"Umm," he said in very low voice.

And for a few minutes, they sat in silence looking at one another in a deferential manner. Neither knew exactly where to take the conversation or the relationship. He was thinking, '*What does she want or need.*' To him, she appeared to be thinking, '*What does he need or want.*' He felt they both were probably thinking of cuddling up somewhere cozy and quiet, with a little music in the background.

The song that popped into his head was a tune by Marvin Gaye & Tammi Terrell, "If I Could Build My Whole World Around You." He imagined that in her head, she was singing a tune by Barbara Mason, '*Yes, I'm Ready.*' He had no idea where that came from, but he could see them holding each other tightly and Walking smoothly across the floor and just submitting to their embrace, not necessarily a precursor to anything more than a sloppy and slobbery kiss.

When they had finished eating, she slid her hands across the table and took his hands, lifted them, and gently kissed them twice. That gesture moved him in some unexpected ways. He was inclined to reciprocate, but instead got up from his side of the table and went and sat next to her. She was breathtakingly beautiful—all over. Her hair was long, black, curly, and shiny—no doubt from creolized parents in Antigua. Because of her short, black skirt, he almost keeled over when he sat next to her—so much of her left thigh and right inner thigh was revealed.

He knew she knew he was checking her out. He also knew that she would wait for him to make a move. He did. The kiss he planted on her muted red lips was the sweetest and smoothest he had witnessed. It was her turn now to make a move. She simply pushed him out of the seat, took his hand, and led him out of the restaurant. With a wave of her right hand, a car pulled up, and she beckoned him to get in the passenger seat while she went to the driver's side and got in.

They rode in silence for about ten miles to the area near downtown Kansas City's East Side in Missouri. The car pulled into the garage of a newly built structure not far from the famed 18th and Vine area. Justin immediately thought about the centrality of this area to the evolution of jazz. The building, a high-rise—twenty-four stories up, was obviously, Justin surmised, part of a burgeoning gentrification of a long-neglected area of Kansas City, and it was clearly a contrast to the nearby low-rise buildings in various states of disrepair. Still, there was a special feeling about the area and about April in tandem that drew him into the Kansas City environs in ways he had neither considered nor anticipated. He was happy, and he was happy to be happy.

She took him to her condominium on the 19th floor of the building. The condominium was a huge four-bedroom affair that swept him deeper into April's world. All of the furniture in the condominium was reminiscent of Scottie's place but decidedly more elegant. All of the furniture was from the Bauhaus school of design: Near an enclosed, modern fireplace housed in a wall in the living room sat two mauve sofas opposite one another and at right angles to the sofas were two love seats of the same style and color. In the center of this arrangement was a large cocktail table that had a black base and a glass top—that sat on top of a white area rug.

In the bedroom, decorated completely in white, was a low bed with chrome legs and a six-foot-high white, leather headboard and king size mattress covered with exquisite white linen. On both sides of the bed were two classically styled Bauhaus tables that were round and sat on bases that were white and of one piece of metal; and on each table sat a glass vase with three white calla lilies. Other rooms in the apartment were similarly decorated—no muss no fuss.

As he watched April move about her space in her simple and short black dress that showed her dazzlingly beautiful legs and inviting behind, he could only move his left hand to his lips to wipe away the slobber that was beginning to form and drip. That was a first for him. He had seen other men engage in that sort of prurient thought, but he felt a little ashamed to find himself doing that. Normally, he would have used one of two white handkerchiefs that he always carried to wipe his lips, but this joy juice came too fast.

April soon walked towards him and handed him a glass of champagne and invited him to sit with her on one of the two love seats facing the fireplace. In that moment, he thought about Florence back in Chicago, but he could only focus there for a few seconds. April's presence demanded that he stay in the moment, and he hesitantly complied.

April said, "You want to be with Florence."

He replied, "Not really. What I want is to revisit a moment in time that I so much enjoyed that I was afraid to repeat it."

April replied, "So why are you inclined to revisit it now."

He took a long sip of champagne and said: "I was afraid Florence would hurt me deeply if I tried to get more from that relationship. With you, I believe that even if you hurt me, it would only be so that I could move to another level of existence or consciousness."

April smiled, but she made no reply.

That time with April that evening was as good as he had anticipated. April was one of the quiet ones who made love as if she were in some creative flow that matched the lines of a Picasso piece or the vibrancy of the colors of a Jacob Lawrence painting. He tried to think of other words or materials or objects to help him capture their lovemaking, but only the images of those two masters came to him. So, as with some other times in the past, he just tried to hold on to the moment as long as he could.

She shifted in the bed, turned over to face him, and said: "You know Scottie told me about you. I want you to know that you met every expectation I held. More than that, you exceeded my expectations!"

He had no response for her except to pull her closer to him, kiss her lightly, hold her butt with his left hand, and fondle her right breast with his right hand. "Umm," he moaned, and he slipped into darkness.

She had breakfast brought in the next morning, and they sat and ate in the "pit" near the fireplace. She sat near him with only his shirt on and sucked on a piece of cantaloupe. She had given him a man's robe to wear, but made no comment about to whom it might belong, if anyone, or whether or not it was an amenity given to any man who spent the night at her place.

When they had almost finished eating, she said: "I am going back to Chicago with you."

He contorted his lips for a second and said: "Alright. You are fully aware of my circumstances, right?"

She replied: "Yes, and I have a plan already in place to make it in Chicago. What time do you want to leave today?"

He replied: "High noon!"

CHAPTER TWELVE

Existential Wandering

As he sat and watched April prepare to accompany him back to Chicago, he thought about how he had always lived his life: Looking for and finding love in all the wrong places and occasionally in the right places. He had no malice in his heart. He just loved women the way the Baptist preacher loves to shout and gesture and hesitate to get the congregation going. His feelings for April had gone far beyond what he felt for Scottie, and that left him in a quandary because Scottie moved him on so many levels of his being.

He retrieved his car and belongings from the hotel where he lodged and then decided to sell it to get money to pay back what he had borrowed to buy the car. As they drove out of Kansas City, he thought to himself, '*Why am I playing in this young woman's life?*' At that same moment, she placed her hand on his thigh and held it tightly. That was comforting, and he laid his head back and dozed off.

Before they started driving, he told her that they could do shifts of one hour in duration. That meant each would only have to drive about 250 miles. That was not a bad deal, but it was still a bit of a burden because he was not a road person. When he finally woke up, she had already driven to St. Louis, half the distance to Chicago.

She said: "I knew you were tired, so I just kept going."

He shook his head and said: "Let's just get a room here for the night and continue in the morning."

She agreed, and they went into the downtown area in search of a luxury hotel. Both seemed to instinctively understand and said to each other that they did not just want to go to any hotel after leaving the splendor of her apartment. After a short period of riding around, they both agreed that the Renaissance hotel was a good place to be.

After they had checked into the hotel, on a whim, they decided to go and see the recently constructed Gateway Arch on the riverfront. Their initial reaction was to stand with their hands in the air and lean towards one another in imitation of the way each leg of the arch appeared to be leaning against and supporting the other leg. That was fun but a little awkward since he was more than seven inches taller than April. She said to him, "That would have been easier with Scottie." He smiled and nodded his head in agreement.

He was ecstatic about having April at his side, but he had started to be preoccupied with how she would survive in Chicago.

So he said, "Tell me about your plan to survive in Chicago."

She replied, "I don't know what I will do specifically to survive, but what I do know is that I have some assets, so to speak, that will make it easy for me to make it in Chicago."

He thought that she was making reference to her physical assets, and he smiled at the thought of her overwhelming beauty and body.

She noticed the smile and continued: "It is not what you are thinking," she said. "I have both a doctor of medicine degree and a doctor of philosophy degree."

He queried: "So you are both an M.D. and a Ph.D.?"

"Yes," she replied. "Are you impressed?"

He pushed his lips out and replied, "Very much so."

She asked him to drive to a restaurant near the hotel that they had selected for the evening. The hotel and restaurant were in a tony neighborhood in St. Louis. With the new information he had about April, he moved about the area with a newfound confidence that bordered on arrogance.

She noticed this but still said, "Let me pay for dinner and the hotel room."

He pulled his lips in slightly and said: "Ok."

He took her hand, and they walked into the restaurant leaning slightly against each other. He wasn't surprised by the recent revelations from April, but he did feel a little bad about the assumptions he had made about her based upon her aggressiveness, clothes, car, and condominium.

He thought to himself: '*St. Louis is one of those big-little towns that feels good as you walk around it, especially the revitalized part of downtown.*' After they ate and returned to the hotel, they got a bottle of champagne and sat and looked out of the hotel window in the direction of the Gateway Arch. They had not talked much about St. Louis, but they both agreed that they could live there. The thought was tempting, and he almost made her an offer he could not refuse.

He told her he would drive the remaining distance to Chicago, and she agreed. The car she drove was a Porsche 912. He had been surprised that she knew how to drive a stick, but based upon recent revelations and time spent with her, going forward, he thought, he would be more surprised if there were things she could not do.

She leaned on his right shoulder as soon as they got in the car and started to immediately snore loudly. He could only smile because it is usually men who are always accused of snoring. His times with women taught him that almost all women snored, especially after a good fuck accompanied by an orgasm.

He was in Chicago's city limits in two and a half hours, which even surprised him. He called a lady friend to see if April could spend the night with her. He was readily accommodated, although he had been intimate with his lady friend. Justin's lady friend made an inquiry about how long April needed a place to be, and he had replied, "Not long."

His lady friend, Sarah, later told Justin that she liked April a lot and welcomed the company for a minute without all of the usual obligatory actions that came when he visited her. He laughed at her candor but did not reply. Sarah was a few years older than Justin, but she remained a good-looking woman, and she had a body that rivaled April's.

April had told Sarah that she would be out of her house in a day or two, but Sarah assured her that she could stay as long as she needed or liked. Sarah also indicated that she thought she would enjoy April's companionship. Although he was not certain, Justin felt that Sarah also found April intellectually and sexually attractive. Justin also felt that spiritually even, Sarah and April appeared to be bound in ways that mystified, scared, and delighted him.

One evening as April and Justin returned from searching for an apartment, Sarah had cooked catfish, greens, corn, and sweet potatoes for them to eat. She had also cooked some muffins made from Jiffy mix. Justin would learn that evening that April had looked for an apartment and a job for twelve hours, four days straight; and she was beginning to feel exhausted.

He thought that a hot meal and a glass of champagne in friendly surroundings was a welcomed respite from the tribulations of the previous four days for April and that day for him. After they had eaten, the three of them decided to sit at the kitchen table and talk.

April said, "I have found an apartment up on the near North side."

Justin thought he saw Sarah grimace and appear to be disappointed at the prospect of April not being in her space anymore. He also thought that Sarah feigned a happy response when she said, "That's great! I am anxious to see what you were able to get. Do you mind if I have a look at your place?"

April said that she was glad to have a Chicagoan offer a second opinion on a newly constructed building called McClurg Court Center, situated across the street from CBS studios and not far from Lake Michigan. The building was bounded by Fairbanks Court to the west, McClurg Court to the east, Ontario Street to the north, and Ohio Street to the south.

Justin decided to leave at that point and kissed each lady as he left.

Continuing their conversation, Sarah said, "Justin told me about your condominium in Kansas City. What's your plan for it?"

April told Sarah that the condominium had been sold weeks before Justin got to St. Louis. Sarah looked puzzled initially, but that was quickly followed by a wry smile. She now had a hint at why she felt a kindred spirit with April.

She said, "You are from Antigua, right?"

It was April's turn to smile and begin to understand why she felt so close to Sarah.

She said, "Yes. And you are too?"

Sarah nodded while now broadly grinning. The two of them stood, walked to each other, and held one another and cried softly for about ten minutes.

Their interlude was interrupted when both finally realized that the phone was ringing in the background that neither had heard when it first started.

Sarah spoke into the phone, "Hello. Oh. Hi, Justin. Yes, April is here. Do you want to speak with her? No? Ok. I will tell her. Goodbye!" She hung up the phone, turned back to April and said: "Justin is going to get us both at eleven in the morning. Apparently, he wants us all to see your place together."

April replied, "Yes. He's excited about the place."

April excused herself by saying, "I am tired. I would like to talk more, but I am exhausted. Would you mind terribly if I retired now?"

Sarah smiled at April's use of words. She involuntarily jerked and then said: "No. I don't mind. I am going to bed, too."

They hugged, pecked each other on the cheek, and held hands briefly before they turned and went in separate directions to their bedrooms.

Justin picked April and Sarah up the next morning and headed for Lake Shore Drive. He knew neither would mind, but he asked April if she had a problem talking in front of Sarah and asked Sarah if she had a problem talking in front of April. They both demurely said, "No."

Justin sensed in that moment that April and Sarah had an unexplored bond that he knew nothing about, but they both wanted to have Justin there to explore that bond—at least part of it.

Justin said, "April, have you told Sarah anything about yourself?"

"Yes," said April. "A little."

Justin tried to guess what "a little" meant, but softly smiled and thought, '*Knowing April, that could be almost nothing or a lot.*' He thought he could have been right either way. What April might have given to Sarah was a huge amount of information about herself if she acknowledged she was from Antigua. On the other hand, he thought, if she had not given to Sarah information about her life here in the United States, which is what Justin was referencing, she had given Sarah nothing.

Justin said to the car, "April is a doctor, a physician. She is also another kind of doctor. She's a doctor of philosophy."

Sarah, who sat in the rear seat behind April by choice, tapped April on the right shoulder and held her hand up to grab April's hand and shake it. Without turning around, April moved her right hand behind her head and held Sarah's hand for several minutes. Justin believed whatever they felt for one another before was now solidified forever. He, too, now felt that bond between April and Sarah, and he delighted in it.

They rode in silence for a few minutes. Justin finally said, "April what is your medical specialty?"

April said, "By training, I am a pediatrician. In practice, I am a pediatrician and a researcher in rare diseases."

Sarah asked, "Why a researcher in rare diseases."

April replied, "When I first went to medical school I just knew I wanted to be a doctor. Later, I choose pediatrics because I thought I would not see the specter of death as often. My aunt Scottie was the person who pushed me hardest to go to college and medical school, and when she told me about some unknown medical condition that episodically came and went for most of her life and would kill her at an early age, I thought I would be able to discover what that disease was and save her life …"

April's voice trailed, and she began to sob. Justin took her hands into his right hand, and Sarah rubbed both of her shoulders gently. As he held April's hand, Justin thought that he got a little of that touching that Sarah gave to April, and to him it felt like it quickly found its way to April's inner-self and spread like water dumped on a dry piece of silk. Justin believed that they all felt something as a result of Sarah rubbing April's shoulders though he did not know the exact source of the feeling or energy or whatever you wanted to call it.

To Justin, it did appear to make them all feel better, and they all seemingly felt a sense of oneness that they had not witnessed as pairs or at any other time in their life. April sat up straight. "I am ok," she said softly. Justin and Sarah continued to touch April diaphanously, and the sense of oneness now seemed to turn into a feeling of vastness that made him feel as if they were all together in Lake Michigan looking up at the sky.

They were sitting safely in front of McClurg Court Center, and he could not remember exactly how they got there after April started to sob. The entrance to the complex was on Ontario, between McClurg Court and Fairbanks Court. He found a parking spot on the street, and he carefully backed in to make sure he did not hit the BMW parked in front of him and the Mercedes-Benz parked behind him.

He sat for a minute to allow April to collect herself. Then he went to the passenger side of the car and opened the front and back door simultaneously, reaching over the back door to help Sarah exit and stealing a look at her luscious inner thighs. He saw April looking at him looking at Sarah's open legs, and as April came up out of the car he saw her open her legs even wider to show him she did not have on any panties. Sweet baby Jesus!

He had not touched either April or Sarah since getting back to Chicago almost a week ago. Now he was slobbering like he did the first time he saw April walking around her condominium. He noticed Sarah watching him, so he pointed to the west and said: "This way."

He was not sure of why he did it, but he moved between April and Sarah, took each one's available hand, and pulled them both close to him. Neither seemed to mind, and that is how they entered the lobby of the building. The doorman apparently remembered April and tipped his hat to acknowledge their entrance.

As they entered the apartment, the sun appeared to peek from behind a cloud to greet them. All three noticed the event and hugged one another at the waist with just a quiet exhalation and peck on the mouth—April and Sarah, unabashedly, did that twice. Justin did not mind, and secretly hoped they would repeat that and do much more. There was something between April and Sarah that went beyond anything he would understand; but as a matter of curiosity, he was hoping that would be revealed to him one day in some way.

The three went about the task of cleaning up the apartment, mostly the detritus left by workers who had painted the apartment, laid down new carpet, and made other final changes to the conformation of the newly constructed space. Soon there were men in the apartment bringing in furniture from design stores and houses such as Design Studio and Roche Bobois. Justin could not stay to see it all come together, but Sarah had already agreed to stay and help April to get her place in order. Justin hugged and kissed both women as he rushed to get to get to his part-time job as a researcher and writer for a Black-owned television production company.

CHAPTER THIRTEEN

Existential Wondering

All of us have some thoughts, wishes, and dreams about how our life will unfold. At some point, however, we all realize that things are not going to happen quite the way we had them visualized. Then comes the period of life when we try to reconcile what is, what was, and what comes next. For Justin, who had always had a vision of his life where he was rich and famous, he knew that he had to leave Betty and the kids and try to enter into some long-term relationship with April. He tried to think about how to make that happen, but a year passed with both of them sort of stuck in a sweet morass of wonderful moments together and painful hours apart with days of emotional limbo pocketing all of it.

April had managed to get a job at Children's Memorial Hospital within a few weeks of arriving in the city. That gave her the security she needed to pursue her passion for research in rare diseases. For that, she was able to secure a gig at the University of Chicago, the premier research institution in the city that specialized in that sort of research by combining many bright young post-doctoral fellows from a broad range of scientific specialties.

Justin sometimes became concerned that in her different work environments, April would find one of the bright young men attractive and want to hook up with him and even perhaps marry and have children. One evening as they lay on the couch after a long, exquisite bit of lovemaking, April said she had something to tell him. His body tensed. He had been here before.

She took his hand and said, "I want us to be under one roof together. I don't want to be married; I just want to have someone to come home to in the evening. Someone to hold me as I drift off to sleep at night."

His reply was, "I will work on that starting tomorrow."

They embraced and, still naked, fell asleep on the couch in her apartment.

When he saw Betty the following evening and stuttered as he tried to tell her he was leaving, she said: "It's okay. Except for passing through to get an occasional change of clothes, you haven't been here with me for a long time. I hate you for what you are doing, but I want space to move on, too. I don't want to fight about this, so let's just fuck one more time before you go and let that be it."

He was surprised by her response to his leaving and was even more surprised as she howled loudly during their lovemaking. That was the first time he heard that primordial scream from a woman entering her orgasmic state. It turned him on like he had never been turned on, and he came twice within a five-minute span. They had not even entirely disrobed before they fell on the floor in the hallway separating the bedroom and the bathroom and started to climb the mountain again to take the plunge down the other side. This time, it was he who howled, and he lost complete consciousness for a moment.

In a half-dressed state, they fell asleep in the hallway for more than an hour. She was the first to awaken, and only smiled as she stared at him and said, "Goodbye." He was able to get dressed in a few minutes.

As he walked to the back door off the kitchen, he took her hand and said: "I'll be back to get my stuff in a few days."

She subtly nodded her head and tried to hold back the tears, which soon flowed gently across her lovely cheekbones. She reached up and kissed him softly on each eye, and then she pecked him on the lips and left the room. She appeared not to want to be a witness to him leaving, although she had told him that she had anticipated the moment for several years before it happened.

April had invited him to stay with her until he found a place for the both of them. She also told him that they could just stay in her place if he was comfortable doing that. He had initially said no to her offer to stay in her place but then said yes after a brief reflection on the matter.

Her place was in many ways the ideal spot for him and the two of them. It was near the lake, which he had always loved in spite of the fact that he could not swim well. It was still near his beloved South Side. It was near almost all of the good restaurants in the city. And there were many spots for them to go dancing or see good plays or good movies. He allowed himself to be drawn closer to April, but not too close because he knew she would one day leave him.

CHAPTER FOURTEEN

I Could Have Loved Her

He continued his work as a high-school history teacher and researcher-writer while April continued to work as a pediatrician and medical researcher. Their combined income allowed them to have a high lifestyle: expensive cars, designer clothes, great food, an extensive range of entertainment experiences, and travel across America and around the world. Life was good. Still, he had an itch that he could not scratch until April said to him one evening, as they sat and read the same novel (*Mumbo Jumbo* by Ishmael Reed), "Why don't you go back to school and finish your doctorate?"

April had helped him locate the area of the itch. He now had to decide if, when, and how he would scratch. He pulled her close and kissed her with a gentleness that was like skating on ice—it was so smooth.

He said, "Thank you, baby. Thank you. I do want to go back and finish the work on my doctorate that I started some years ago. Right now, however, I want to sit here and just read this novel with you. I love the exchange we have around shared experiences. It always makes me feel closer, more intimate with you."

April smiled and nodded her head in agreement. She moved closer and up under him to get a better snuggle. The itch was gone.

That next day he walked into the Office of Admissions at the School of Education at the University of Chicago and told the secretary behind the long counter that stretched the length of the room that he was there to complete an application for readmission to the School of Education's doctoral program. She stared at him for a moment, then rose without a word, stepped towards him, reached into one of several boxes on the counter in front of him, and handed him a form to fill out.

She finally spoke, saying: "After you fill that out, I will see if the Dean can talk with you now. Good luck!"

There was no place to sit or stand to complete the form, but he remembered seeing a desk and chair in the hall outside of the Office of Admissions. He went into the hall, and after about fifteen minutes, he returned to the secretary with an outstretched hand and completed form.

She took the form, reviewed it quickly, and said: "Please have a seat. I will see if Dean Bern can see you now."

After a short while, Dean Bern appeared in the doorway of his office and beckoned him to come in. After a warm greeting and in an invitation to have a seat, the Dean told him he was sure he could return to the university to complete his doctoral studies but that there were a few conditions for his return.

First, he would have to complete an additional fifteen hours of graduate courses. Second, he would have to submit an essay indicating why he wanted to return to finish his doctorate at this time. Third, he would have to go before a committee in a different concentration than what he had been in because that concentration had recently been eliminated. Fourth, he would have to submit possible topics for his dissertation. And, finally, he would have to provide the names of four faculty members who might serve on his dissertation committee.

Dean Bern then sat back in his chair to wait for a response. In the interim, he said. "The good news is that we have a particular grant program now that will pay for all of your courses and expenses related to you pursuing your Ph.D. I understand from the Department's secretary that you still have money you can get from the federal and state governments related to time served in the Army. That ought to make your decision easy."

It did. He tried to imagine being in a classroom again with students ten or fifteen years his junior, but even that had a particular appeal. He asked the Dean about deadlines and other specifics, but most of what he got from the Dean was simply, "See the Department's secretary when you leave today." After a twenty-minute conversation with the secretary, he left Hutchins Common with a high that he had known before and in which he delighted. He thought to himself, '*I will cook dinner for April tonight and bring in a nice bottle of champagne.*'

As April stepped into the apartment and saw the small candles flickering, smelled the baked salmon cooking, and looked at him broadly smiling, she said: "You are back in school. That is wonderful. I am happy for you. I have known for some time that you needed to do that. Let's eat."

After an embrace that made them both deliriously giddy, he held her chair and gestured for her to come and eat and celebrate the moment of his return to a part of him that had been ignored for a while.

He had chilled the champagne glasses in the freezer; added barbecued shrimp to the baked salmon; cooked home fries with fresh onions and herbal and garlic salts; sautéed fresh green beans with onions, fresh mushrooms, and fresh bell peppers of various hues; and baked an apple pie from scratch. April took in all of that and gave him that smile that seemingly said, "I got something for you, boy!"

He looked at April and said: "I am glad you are in my life. I like you, girl!"

As they ate, he talked about his time at the University that day and what would be required of him to finish his doctorate. April smiled, kissed him gently, and said: "Piece of cake for you." He nodded his head in agreement although there was a new bit of heaviness on one of his shoulders.

Making love that evening was all that each had expected and more. As they lovingly held one another and drifted in and out of sleep, April said: "This is also a good time for you to pursue that other thing we talked about in Kansas City.

He trembled a little, and replied: "I know."

April said, "Then you also know that I am with you, right?"

"Yes," he replied, "Yes."

Holding hands and smiling, they lost a level of consciousness that allowed them to enter the next day still holding hands. Neither spoke as they lay in bed that Saturday morning now aware of the fact that they were still holding hands from the night before.

He said, "I don't want to get all philosophical on you because I am now back at the University, but I think I know what it means to be able to speak to my soul."

April smiled, and Justin thought she might be saying to herself: '*Not exactly the way I wanted to start the morning, but let me stay in the moment since I started this, sort of.*'

But she said out loud, "Oh. Let me hear."

He did not yet have the clarity that he wanted to speak now about a matter he had only periodically thought about for the last four or five years, but he understood the value of speaking and writing as a way of getting clarity about a variety of matters.

So he began: "Part of my being able to speak to my own soul has to do with completing my doctorate. That's something I have wanted and needed as long as I can remember. Another part has to do with writing a book that comes out of that experience, which does not have any meaning because I have yet to go through that experience. So on that matter, I have almost no clarity. Any other part or parts of my learning to speak to my soul, I am not sure about yet. What I am sure about is that I am on the right track."

April nodded her head gently several times and said: "I can leave you now. I have met a fellow at the hospital who wants to marry me and have a large family. I am not sure about the large family, but I am sure about having a few kids and a family, and probably living somewhere in the far North or South suburbs. You do understand, don't you?"

He replied, "When do you plan to do all of this?"

She replied: "Soon."

Within a few months, April had sublet the apartment, married a White doctor from the hospital where she worked, and moved to Oakbrook, a suburb west of Chicago. They parted company as amicably as they had met.

She had only one question: "Will you always love me as much as you love Scottie?"

He did not reply, but rocked his head and body back and forth to acknowledge her question and to signify to her, "Yes."

Each wanted to stay, but both recognized they had to go. He held back his tears as long as he could, but as soon as her taillights disappeared, he began to sob uncontrollably. That was harder than he thought it would be. He wanted to stop for a drink in one of the local bars near the apartment complex but opted instead to return to his apartment on 82nd and South Parkway where he had only lived for a few days.

CHAPTER FIFTEEN

Love and Choices

He applied for and got a job as a dean at Loop Community College, one of the City Colleges of Chicago. He was dean of the evening school, which gave him some flexibility for occasionally attending classes at the University of Chicago's campus during the afternoon and morning. It had been some time since he had sat in a class, but he found the experience exhilarating as he competed with the professors for the attention of students about matters in the books and the real world.

He understood that the professors might have more knowledge than he did about the theory or theories of education, but he was sure he knew more than the professors about the practices of education. It was a fine line between contributing robustly to discussions and being arrogant about how much he knew about the practices of education. Occasionally, he thought he felt and saw some professors bristle a bit after he had made a comment; but for the most part, he felt confident that he only brought useful information and clear insights to the class discussions.

Several young ladies in his classes winked and blinked at him to get his attention, but he was not inclined to do more than look at them and smile. He missed April, and he did not want to use anybody to distract him from his deeply felt void: What was she doing? Where was she? Was she pregnant yet? Did she love her husband as much as she loved him? How close was she to finding a cure for her aunt's disease? Did she and Sarah stay in touch? Would he find another woman that matched him so well in so many ways?

Over several years at the University, he did have several affairs of varying duration and intensity. One of those affairs was with a doctor and professor at the school of medicine. Interestingly enough, he had been introduced to her by April who had called him just to inquire about his well-being.

She had started the conversation with him by saying, "Do you miss me? Do you have a new lady in your life?"

To which he had replied, "Yes, I miss you. No, I do not have a new lady in my life."

After that initial exchange, they continued to talk about matters in general, until she said: "I have a friend who is a professor in the school of medicine at Chicago and a physician at the hospital there. Would you like to meet her?"

He replied, "Yes. When?"

She said, "This Friday. My husband and I thought it would be nice if we could find a date for Nicole and go out to dinner."

He said, "Why me?"

She replied, "Alfred likes you. He respects you, and he is comfortable with the way you have handled our relationship and the way it ended. And, no. He is not looking for a ménage à trios."

To which he replied: "What about you? Are you looking for a ménage à trios?"

There was silence on the line for a few moments, and then April replied, "Possibly."

He smiled at that response because he knew that was an affirmative. So he said, "How do you want to get together?"

She said, "We will get you at 6:30 P.M. We are going to dinner at the Le Bastille. Have you eaten there?"

He quickly said, "Yes." But he did not elaborate.

April said, "Good. See you on Friday."

Although they had talked by phone probably once a month for several years, neither he nor April tried to move outside of the initial boundaries they had set for their relationship after she was married. She said her husband was aware of their past relationship and the fact that they still communicated with one another. She said she never gave him any reason not to trust her, and she had found no reason not to trust him.

At some level, he felt betrayed by both her comments and the fact that she had left him to pursue her dreams and life. He understood, however, that what she did was pretty much predetermined. It was for him another one of those times he wished that he could hold onto but couldn't.

When April called and told him that they were on the way to get him, he was not sure just how or what he was feeling. He wanted to meet Nicole, although April had not given him any information about her. He also wanted to meet Alfred, April's husband and the man who had pulled April out of his orbit and into his. That thought hurt a bit. He was anxious for the evening to get underway, and he went to the lobby of his apartment immediately after April called even when knowing that he had a ten-minute wait.

Nicole was in the car already when it pulled up in front of the building. It was a four-door Silver Bentley. The beauty of the car did not surprise him, but he was very surprised by the beauty of the women who stepped out of the car to greet him standing up.

She smiled at him and said, "April was right. You are a cutie-pie."

He blushed a bit, an unusual response for him. He, in turn, said, "Yes, we all seem to be variations on a theme."

Nicole emitted a hearty laugh and said, "I am going to like you, sir."

Before they moved towards the restaurant, Alfred extended his hand to Justin and said, "April has told me a lot about you. I am glad to be finally able to meet you."

His reply was, "Yes. I have heard about you, too. It's a pleasure to meet you."

With that exchange over, there was silence in the car for a few minutes, which was broken by Nicole who said, "What can I expect at this restaurant?"

Justin said, "Good food, a lively atmosphere, and a lot of fun given the company you are in."

Everybody chuckled at the comment. Then Nicole decided to slide across the seat to be nearer to him. Never lost for a response to most things, Justin slid closer to her and placed his leg across the hump on the floor of the car so that it touched Nicole's leg. She smiled and put her hand on his knee as a way of approving of his move.

He thought to himself, '*Nothing slow about this woman.*'

Alfred said, "There it is. Looks interesting."

April mumbled, "More than you think."

There was valet parking, but Alfred told the valet that he would valet park only if he could take the car to the place where it would be parked.

At first, the valet did not understand what was being asked of him, but he finally said, "Ok. Just park it in the space across the street there. I will keep an eye on it."

The valet stood and watched Alfred make a U-turn and return to the side of the street where they all stood waiting. Justin had given the valet money, and April beckoned to Alfred to follow her.

He wasn't sure how much April knew about Le Bastille or what he and Florence had done in that space. He did not know, and he did not care. There was a little residual malignancy that he felt in his heart towards April that had all to do with her now being married and settled in a new home with new children and a new husband. No. That was not it. He felt some hatred for April because of what she did. A deep longing to hold her and to be held by her accompanied that hatred. To distract him from those thoughts, he reached and grabbed Nicole's hand and guided her into the restaurant.

He resisted at first, but he felt himself being drawn into the evening with a feeling of happiness that he had not had for a while. Alfred was a nice dude: Intelligent, good-looking, gregarious, and even charming in some ways. Nicole was a stunning woman in many respects: Short blonde hair, chiseled features, ample bust and butt, lovely legs, intelligent, and extremely outgoing. And, of course, April: A little bit heavier now (maybe 10 or 11 pounds), slightly more gregarious than he remembered her to be, black as ever, and prettier than ever. She still had him.

The three of them tried to steer away from professional talk, but invariably some topic related to medicine dominated the conversation. At one point in the evening, it was the newly discovered AIDS that dominated the conversation. He decided to take the conversation back to April and her search for what killed her aunt. April seemed anxious to enter that discussion.

She started with, "Research in the area of DNA appears to be one of the most promising directions for what I am interested in." She went on to explain that DNA held the genetic code for almost all living things and that scientists were just beginning to understand the relationship between the code, various diseases, and species/individual characteristics.

He saw her continue to speak, but he did not hear much of what she said. He was in her rapture, and Nicole pushed her leg up against his to bring him back to the gathering. Nicole had also copped an attitude that made him like her a bit more.

He thought to himself, '*She doesn't even know me. What's the attitude about?*'

As if she had heard his thought, she leaned over and whispered to him: "Jesus. Can I have at least one man at the table admire me and want to get in my draws? April is gorgeous and sexually attractive, but so am I. What's the deal?"

The deal was really simple, and he thought to himself: '*April's beauty and persona transcended every standard held for beauty and personas in America: She had black hair, black skin, dark eyes, big ass, big bust, big and gorgeous legs, and full lips. Add to that an ebullient personality that was mostly like an iceberg: only 10 percent of the total surface was usually seen, which made her appear aloof and reserved to most people. That was the deal, and it was usually men who were most fascinated by April's existence. Only a few women got to see what April was about.*'

He whispered to Nicole: "You know what the deal is, but I will talk to you about it later."

As the evening wore on, Justin thought that Nicole seemed increasingly less interested in what was happening at the table. She appeared to be ready for the evening to end, at least that part of it that involved both couples. He thought that she had another agenda, and it was probably about wanting to know more about this motherfucker next to her who all but ignored her to look at and slobber over the Black bitch across the table from her. He was sure that Nicole did not mean April any harm. He felt that Nicole was just invidious of what April was able to do with a Black man and a White man while she was in their midst.

Justin thought that Nicole probably thought to herself, '*Oh, how the mighty have fallen.*'

As they left the restaurant, Nicole pulled Justin close and kissed him on the mouth, which he thought was nice. He smiled and attempted to kiss her, but she turned away. He thought to himself: '*Game time.*' But the moment they were in the car with Alfred and April, she kissed him again. This time, the kiss was much longer, and even April noticed it.

April said, "He is a good kisser. Probably the best in the world."

That comment made the car fill with laughter, and Justin thought that it was partly in recognition of some truth and partly to remove tension from the car that came from the kissing and the comment about the kissing. Nicole quickly said she wanted to go to the BBC, a disco up on Division Street, not far from where they were. April and Alfred begged off by saying they had to get the kids to soccer games and piano lessons early Saturday morning.

Nicole said she and Justin would get cabs home without a problem. Alfred told April to go with Justin and Nicole and that he would take care of the kids with the help of the nanny.

When April asked, "But how will I get home?"

Alfred replied, "Just drop me at the METRA and take the Bentley. I will get a cab from the train station."

Justin was delighted at the turn of events. He liked Alfred even more now. He had thought only a brother could have made that kind of response to the world.

He shook hands and embraced Alfred as if he were a brother, and whispered: "I will make sure she is safe and gets home fairly soon."

Alfred did not verbally respond, but he did nod his head slightly.

They drove a few blocks south and west to the METRA station. April walked Alfred to the ticket booth in the train station, and after Alfred had appeared to be on the train and on the way home, she returned to the car and asked Justin to drive. He agreed, and the three of them climbed in the front seat together. He was quiet, but effervescent inside.

Nicole suddenly appeared to be deliriously happy. She talked about how great it was for just the three of them to be together, and how happy she was she had agreed to come out with them for the evening, and how much she liked dancing, and how she wanted a real cold glass of champagne.

April, initially silent, broke out into a song for a few seconds. She then reached into the glove compartment and took out a tape by the Whispers. She forwarded the tape to a tune called "Hello Stranger," a remake of a Barbara Lewis' tune from the mid-60s. On this one, it had Carrie Lucas leading the group with the smooth Whispers singing background.

April told Justin to pull over. She then showed him how to open the convertible top on the Bentley. She started over the song that had been playing, and now they all knew the song and the refrain, especially the part that went: "shoo-bop, shoo-bop, my baby, ooh."

Justin thought that they all appeared to be surprised at how good they sounded, although they had much help from the music playing in the car. He also thought that Nicole now seemed to be over the top. Whatever funk she had been in because of April and the responses being made to her in the restaurant, it appeared now to be gone. When the guitar riff started about three-quarters of the way through the song, now being played for the fourth time, they all played air guitars and sang to try and make the sound of the guitar: duh duh duh duh duh duhhh, duh duh duhhh.

At the disco, they were shuffled to the front of the line and immediately let in. None of them appeared to know why they got in so quickly. Was it the Bentley, Nicole, April, or him? That conversation quickly ended, and they had a bottle of champagne brought to the table where they had been seated. He told them to give him their money and valuables out of their purses, and he stuffed it all in his pants and coat pockets.

When the extended version of Blondie's "Rapture" started, he asked them both to join him on the dance floor. April declined and watched as he and Nicole went dancing to the heavy beat of the music and dizzying lights of the disco. When they returned, April was gone. Neither was inclined to talk about April's leaving, so they spent the rest of the night drinking champagne and dancing. During the evening, he did occasionally wonder about April's safety, but they had valet parked, so he did not stay there long.

At about 3:00 A.M. in the morning, Justin and Nicole left the disco and went to her apartment in Marina City, an iconic structure on the north branch of the Chicago River in downtown Chicago. Nicole told him that she had chosen that complex solely on the basis of the exterior, which looked like stacked flying saucers, and the interior, which had few right angles. Her apartment looked like a slice of pie, with the kitchen and bathroom near the skinny part and the bedroom and living room at the big end, both of which opened out to a huge balcony and a fabulous view of the city. Her apartment had a river view and a view of downtown Chicago.

Neither of them was inclined to do more than climb into bed and go to sleep; backs turned to one another. In the middle of the night, they did wake up and make love with a slowness and tenderness that neither had had for a long time.

Before falling back to sleep, he told her, "I needed that."

She responded, "Me, too."

In an instant, they were both again sound asleep and calling hogs. In the morning, without speaking, they just went at it again, hoping that the neighbors would not hear them in the noise of the day.

Justin felt that they both were satiated by the time the sun started to go down. They appeared to be hungry, too. She offered to have food brought up from one of the restaurants in the building. He offered to pay for the meal or, at least, split the bill, but she declined his offer. They ate rib-eye steaks (rare for her and well-done for him), home fries, and asparagus (with a sauce of some kind). They also shared a triple-layered piece of chocolate cake with just a little Haagen-Dazs vanilla ice cream. She had had the Veuve brut champagne already chilled. They had finished two bottles by the time they decided to go out for the evening.

As they dressed to go out for the evening, the phone rang. Nicole answered and mouthed April's name to him. April wanted to come by and hang with them for the evening. They both smiled and quickly nodded in agreement to April's request. April offered to bring Justin one of Alfred's clean white shirts and a tie that she had picked out.

He smiled at the thought of that and said, "Great."

Nicole seemed to be okay with the prospect of April joining them for the evening, but he still asked: "How do you feel about April coming along this evening."

She said, "I'm good with that. It should be fun, especially for you."

He thought to himself, '*Nicole, you could have kept that last bit.*'

He said to her, "Yea, I like that as a notion," though he was not inclined to define or elaborate on what he meant by "notion." He had not elaborated on the word "notion" because he had not given it a great deal of thought. So he said to himself, '*What did I mean by that?*' Nothing much came to mind in the instant he asked himself the question, but shortly after that, he was grinning to himself. The notion was not a single notion, but a bevy of images—of him and April together, then him and Nicole together, then the three of them together, and then April and Nicole together. Whew!

Staring at Justin sardonically, Nicole said: "Despite our evening and day together, you still can't get April out of your mind even after not being with her for several years."

He replied, "That's true. You want to make it just about love and sex between April and me. It is more. Much more, and I don't think we have time for me to explain it to you even if I were inclined. So, for the moment just let me say this: Surprisingly, you moved me in some ways that April never did. And we don't have time to talk about that, either. My thoughts just now were not just about being with either of you. They were about being with both of you, individually and together. They were also about the two of you being together."

Nicole's smile at that point was wider than the Jack Nicholson's Joker's smile in the Batman movie, and Justin knew he had Nicole. Her being with April was something she had apparently entertained independent of his thoughts on the matter.

So Justin just turned and headed for the shower. When he showered, he had to suppress all thoughts about both Nicole and April, but he did mutter to himself something about life being good. The heavens did not open, and the choir did not gloriously sing in that moment, but bliss was on his shoulder and in his hand.

Nicole called to him, "April is on her way up."

Justin scurried to be ready to receive April in his best form, but he forgot that April had the shirt and tie he needed to be fully ready. He exhaled, pulled a tight-fitting black tee shirt over his head, slipped into a pair of black Levi jeans, and pulled his stomach in to make it appear that he was still svelte.

Still barefooted, he stepped into the room where both April and Nicole sat drinking champagne. They both smiled, and each reached over and rubbed the arm of the other. In chorus, they said, "Ooh," and then laughed. For the second time within a few days, he blushed, and then sat down between them. Nicole passed him the glass of champagne they had poured for him.

They talked about where they would go for the evening. A lot of names were tossed out, and the suggestions were finally narrowed to two: One suggestion was Coconuts up on Sheridan Road, but the consensus was Dingbats on Ontario. Coconuts was an exciting scene, but the music played there was just okay. They had all been to Coconuts, but no one had been to Dingbats, which had transitioned from a White venue to a gay venue to a Latino venue to a hot spot frequented mostly by Blacks and a variety of folks. The music mix there was somewhat eclectic: disco, R & B, pop, rock, and blues. That in and of itself made it the place to go and be.

April insisted that they take the Bentley, thinking that would get them into the club quicker. And when they drove up to Dingbats, formerly called Tenemant Square, they were immediately greeted like celebrities and escorted to the front of the long line of patrons waiting to enter the club. Both April and Justin glanced at one another and smiled because they immediately recognized that they had once shared an apartment in McClurg Court right across the street from Dingbats.

The first thing they saw as they entered the club was this huge Black guy, later to be known as Mr. T. Justin had heard that before Mr. T's tenure as head bouncer at Dingbats for several years, there had been occasional fights between patrons of the club, but his presence seemed to quell much of that. But Justin always thought Mr. T's presence might have been only part of the reason for the calm that was part of the night scene at Dingbats and other clubs. The other reason was the trance-like states produced by the drugs and music that were part of the disco scene.

Justin ordered champagne for the group and an extra glass for Alfred—more symbolic than anything else. April smiled at the gesture and grabbed his hand and pulled him to the dance floor. As he danced frenetically with April and watched her body move in ways he had not seen before, he felt himself slobber in the same way he had done when they were in her condominium in Kansas City. This time, he was able to get one of his pristine, white handkerchiefs from his right back pocket and wipe his mouth before he made a fool of himself.

April did not help him. She moved closer to him and pulled him in between her legs and moved up and down with such sensuous moves that he alternated between feeling that he wanted to faint and feeling that he wanted to ravish or ravage her, probably more the latter for her leaving him at a moment when he most loved her. Before either of those things occurred, he saw Nicole tap April on the shoulder to get her turn to dance with him. He only slightly exhaled, but he felt an even deeper affinity for Nicole. In that moment, she had rescued him from either the most embarrassing situation of his life or the most calamitous one. In either case, he was grateful—really grateful.

After about twelve more minutes of jumping up and down, Justin and Nicole returned to the table. April had again disappeared without saying goodbye. They just shrugged their shoulders slightly, drank three more glasses of Champagne, and then returned to the dance floor for the next forty-five minutes straight. They both now had a buzz, and they entered a trance-like state that only a combination of alcohol, music, dancing, and the possibility of mind-blowing sex can take you to.

When he got Nicole home in bed, he attacked her with all of the ferocity that he held in his heart for April and all of the love and lust he felt for Nicole. They both howled for hours, and they woke up on the floor in the living room the next morning totally spent from the activities of the previous evening.

Neither appeared inclined to talk at first, but Nicole finally said: "Was that for April or me?"

He replied, "Both."

He saw Nicole smile and said to himself, '*She knew that.*'

CHAPTER SIXTEEN

Starting and Stopping

He and Nicole ran the streets of Chicago and other world-class cities for the next five years, but one evening she announced, after a great session of making love, that she, like April, had to go. She wanted the house in the suburbs, the husband, children, and dog. Neither had seen or talked to April for quite awhile, but they both often thought of her and mentioned her in their conversations.

She slowly continued, "I have met a Black man at the hospital, and he wants to make an honest woman out of me. I know that sounds corny, but he wants to marry me and give me what April has. In fact, he already owns a house not too far from where April lives in Oakbrook and has talked about us moving there after we get married."

Justin thought to himself: '*What is it about women and me. They seem to love me, deeply. But I am not a choice for a forever mate. Or else they get silly and I have to go.*'

As if she had heard his thoughts, Nicole said, "It's not that I don't love you or don't want to be with you. I just have the feeling that marriage is not a state of mind or being you want to climb back into. And I get that. So I am just thinking we should break it off while it is still good to us and I am still attractive enough to get a man I want and can love and who loves and wants to marry me."

He hadn't seen that one coming. But he was able to embrace her and whisper: "I understand. Invite me to the wedding."

He dressed and returned to his apartment that evening. For several days, he was unable to sleep or eat much. But after several weeks, he was feeling better, especially after he got back out in the world. He was not invited to the wedding, and he had no intention of going if he had been. But he had good memories of Nicole and April.

He had always thought a ménage a trois with him, April, and Nicole would be the ultimate in sex if not intimacy. But somehow he never seriously thought to pursue that because, at some level, he felt it would be disrespectful and unfulfilling to all of them. Both April and Nicole were women that required a man's total attention all of the time and all of the way, especially in the bed.

After Nicole had left his life, there were many days that followed when he was still trying to wrap his mind around the idea and memory of another lady that he dearly loved leaving him in tears. He was the one that had chosen, after a previous marriage and affairs of varying durations and intensity over the years, to leave the streets and settle down with a wife and have kids. Or at least, he had agreed to that arrangement, an oddity in itself because he had never asked any of his ladies to marry him. They had either asked him to marry or after a conversation made that the basis for them being together.

Although he had never asked a woman to marry him, he had known women that he almost married simply because the relationship was that good. He had met one of the women he almost married at the community college where he now worked. She was walking down the hall one afternoon during the summer when the sun was still bright and warm.

He didn't remember why he had looked up at that moment; but when he did, he saw her coming towards him with the sun at her back. Whatever she was wearing somehow allowed the sun to cast a halo around her and to show most of her body in a silhouette that revealed a fabulous shape that stopped him from moving and sent his heart racing and his body shaking. In that moment the heavens did open, and the choir did sing a magnificent version of Handel's "Hallelujah Chorus."

He returned to his office more stimulated by that apparition than anything he had witnessed in all of his time here on earth. He had to find her and find out who she was. As soon as he asked his secretary if she knew this woman that he could only describe in general terms such as short, light-skinned, beautiful, big afro, nice shape, and lovely smile; the secretary gave him a name: Haley Powell.

The secretary added, "Everybody knows Haley. She's in the science department and teaches biology. She has taught here for five years. She is married and has four children."

His heart slowed, his moments of extreme exaltation came crashing down, and he found himself in his office with the door closed and his head on his desk without remembering precisely how he got there. He stood up and walked to the window in his office to look at some of the new buildings being put up in the downtown area. After a few minutes of wondering just how those buildings could rise so high in the sky, he decided to look for Haley and ask her to lunch.

He found Haley in her office. He knocked on the open door and was told to come in.

He walked in and said: "Hi, my name is Justin. I am the assistant dean in the Applied Sciences division. Would you like to go to lunch with me now?"

Haley smiled and quickly said, "Yes. Give me a moment to gather my things."

He was somewhat surprised at Haley's quick and affirmative response, but he also knew that women liked men who were bold and confident— bordering on arrogance. He had already picked out a restaurant in a boutique hotel not far from the college, and since it was warm they decided to walk there.

As soon as they sat down in a booth in the restaurant, she said: "What do you want?"

He hadn't expected that question so soon, but he quickly replied: "You."

Haley laughed and said, "But are you sure you can handle me?"

He hesitated and then said: "No. But it should be fun for both of us to see if I can."

Haley's smile diminished considerably for a moment and then flashed sensuously. She then said: "I don't know about you, but I don't have any more classes today."

He replied, "I am an administrator. I don't have any classes period."

Haley's smile became even more sensuous, and she said: "Why don't you get a room here in the hotel for the afternoon and show me what you got."

He smiled and almost ran away. He was out there now and decided it was do or die.

He rose from the table and said, "I will be right back."

In a few minutes, he returned to the table and gently offered a hand to help her come out of the booth. He continued to hold her hand as they took the elevator to the 35ᵗʰ floor and a room that was facing east and north towards the lake and downtown area. Neither spoke as they unabashedly disrobed and stood hugging and kissing one another tenderly.

The extreme exaltation that he had earlier felt and lost returned with such a force that his knees buckled a bit. Haley moaned and intensified her kissing before they both fell on the bed in a sweet and tremulous embrace that he had not felt for a very long time.

In that moment, he did not care that his secretary was probably looking for him or that Haley was married with four children. The only thing that mattered for both of them in that moment was being together in a room and trying to reach the heavens, already facilitated somewhat by being in a building that tried to do the same.

Because she was so petite and shapely, he was able to wrap his left arm around her and rub her left nipple gently and thrust deeply into her. She looked up at him and smiled, and then she closed her eyes and started to moan in a way that made him join her. In that contorted position, noisy rapture, and uncontrollable convulsions of their bodies, they fought to stay on the conscious side of an orgasm. That was a battle they soon lost as she cried and screamed and he lost consciousness for a period of time longer than he had ever done. It was dark when they woke up.

He said, "Don't you have to hurry home and get your kids."

She said, "No. My mother has the kids, and my husband is in the military, so he is not even here in the United States. And even if he were here, it would not matter. I will tell you more about that later."

They both dressed; and after only a few minutes, they were on Lake Street headed back to the college. For a moment they held hands, but then recognized that might not be appropriate yet. On the elevator up to their respective offices, they did steal a sweet and tender kiss.

There were no promises of anything beyond that afternoon, but he knew and felt that Haley knew that they would see one another again. As she departed the elevator, she waved over her shoulder at him without ever turning around to look at him. He smiled at that move, and thought to himself: '*Absolutely lovely,*' as he watched her switch her fine behind off the elevator.

He got a call a few days later from Haley, and she asked if they could just go to dinner and talk for a bit after work. He agreed and asked if she wanted him to make the reservation.

She replied, "No. I have done that already. It is in the same restaurant where we ate the first time we met. Is 7:00 P.M. good for you?"

He said, "Yes. I will meet you on the Lake Street side of the college at 6:45. It is a beautiful evening so we can walk to the restaurant if you don't mind?"

As they walked to the restaurant, a warm, light breeze came from the lakefront, and they reflexively reached for one another's hand. He told her that he had thought about her often in the time they were apart, but he had decided to wait for her to call since she was in the most tenuous position.

She told him that she had thought about him often, too, but wanted time to think about where she wanted a relationship with him to go. She told him that she would like to have him as a lover; perhaps a companion; and perhaps something even more. She wasn't sure, but she was sure she did not want him just to slip away. So she had called him that day.

When they reached the restaurant, a gentleman who had a knowing smile greeted them and led them to a secluded area of the restaurant.

He told them, "Your waitress is Mary. She should be with you shortly."

Although there was room to sit across from one another, they chose to sit next to each other in one corner of the booth to which they had been shown. He thought to himself, '*God. She is even lovelier than I remember.*'

Just then, the waitress appeared and greeted them. She told them about the specials for the day and made an inquiry about the kinds of drinks they might want. Haley asked for a Kir Royal, and he ordered plain champagne.

They sat for a moment in silence, and then each reached for the hand of the other without a word spoken. She then said, "Tell me about yourself. I don't see a ring, so I assume you are not married. Do you have a steady girlfriend?"

He told her that he did not have a steady girlfriend although he had dated several ladies who were kind enough not to push for more than that. He did not tell the other part—that they both left him because they wanted the dream almost all women wanted. He also added that he had only been intimate with one of the ladies at a time.

Haley smiled at that last bit of information and replied: "So you are just one of those confirmed bachelors?"

He replied, "No. I have been married. It just did not work out."

She replied, "Would you get married again?"

He said, "Yes. If the right woman asked me."

Haley bellowed at that response and said: "Cute. I will remember that. What would the right woman have to be like and act like?"

He quickly said, "You."

She frowned and said, "Is that it? Tell me what that means."

He had sat for a minute before he spoke, but he finally said: "She would have to be intelligent and probably educated, more the former than the latter. She would have to have a moral center that doesn't have to emanate from any religion, although that would not be a problem if it did. She would have to be good looking and well-built—nicely shaped legs and breasts. She also would have to know when to start and stop."

Haley stared at him intently for about twenty seconds and then finally said: "What does knowing when to start and stop mean? When to start and stop doing what?"

He replied, "Everything. Talking, kissing, smiling, working, playing, fucking, and so on."

Haley demurely smiled and said, "Got you." She then took his hands between hers, and repeated: "Got you." With that, she rose and said: "Is that an expectation, advice, an admonition, or garbage."

He replied quickly: "A wish—for myself and anyone who is in my orbit."

Haley sat back down and said: "Let's order dinner and talk a bit more."

CHAPTER SEVENTEEN

Love's Lament

It was easy to be with Haley, but there was a slight discomfort in their relationship that he could not put his finger on. Whenever they were together, she could make that discomfort easily dissipate by kissing him lightly and playing with his nipples. Sex did not automatically follow such moments, but it often did. Even when it did not, he found the noise inside of him quieted when she made that move. One evening after making love that had been preceded by Haley's titillating moves, the noise inside of him got louder instead of dissipating. So he said to her: "Tell me about your husband."

Her lips pushed out a bit, and she said: "He's a general in the Air Force. He started as an enlisted man and rose through the ranks quickly. He was an infantryman when he first joined the armed forces. He served in Germany and Tokyo. We have spent more time apart than together over the last twenty years. He would appear on my doorstep every three or four years, screw me enough times for me to get pregnant, and then he was gone as soon as I would announce that I was pregnant. Before he went in the Air Force, he was a lieutenant colonel in the Army. Just in case you are wondering, you are not the first lover I have taken in the interludes of my marriage: Sort of interludes within interludes."

Haley paused and said: "You don't like that last comment."

To which he replied: "Uh. I am not sure I like or dislike that last remark. I am trying to be free of judging you for how you see the world or what you have done or do in the world. We all have to find our own way in this life, and if we do no harm to others, at least intentionally, I honestly don't see the problem."

Haley looked at him with a half smile and said: "Sometimes you are just too intellectually smug for me."

He looked at her and said: "You are right. What I am feeling and thinking is that you should have made a choice to either be in or out of your marriage. The first time your husband went away without taking you with him, you should have asked that he make a choice to be in your life or not in your life. Am I still being intellectually smug?"

To which she replied: "Yes, I think you are still being intellectually smug, and you have added to that the fact that you are now also being morally smug. Get away from me!"

Haley grabbed her purse and rushed from the restaurant. She hailed a cab that went north on State Street. He had never known where she lived, and he had assumed that it was on the South Side somewhere. He sat in the restaurant for an hour after Haley left, and he tried to think about what had gone wrong in his conversation with Haley. He recognized that he was sometimes stupidly arrogant, but both of them had acknowledged and talked about that. What else was it that perhaps he had missed that pissed Haley off?

He paid the tab for the food and drinks they had, and then he decided to return to his office to do some work to take his mind off the matter. At about 8:30 P.M. his office phone rang, and Haley said: "I am sorry. You did nothing to deserve my outburst and my leaving you without at least saying goodbye. Again, I apologize."

For a moment, there was dead silence on the phone, but he was able to get out: "Thank you. I don't know that there is a need for you to apologize, but I do feel better now that you have offered one. Can we get together tomorrow and talk a little bit more about it?"

She said, "Yes. I would like for you to take me to another restaurant for dinner at five. Does your schedule permit you to do that?"

He replied, "Yes. See you at four forty-five at the Lake Street entrance."

He liked Haley a lot. It had not been his intent to offend her, but he now better understood her question to him when they first met: "But are you sure you can handle me?" He had initially thought about the question in strictly sexual terms, but he now understood that Haley meant something far different from that—perhaps in addition to that but much, much more.

As they sat across from each other in an Italian restaurant on Wacker and Michigan Avenues, he found himself biting his bottom lip and not saying much. They had already exchanged salutations and engaged in other social pleasantries in front of the college and while they walked to the restaurant. Now each seemed to wait for the other to start a pleasant if not meaningful exchange between them.

He blinked first and said: "It is my turn to apologize to you for being such an asshole. Sometimes I get all sophomoric because I get some of that in my classes at the university, but there is no malice when I do that. It is sort of a warm-up to a more meaningful conversation for the most part."

Haley raised her eyebrows and smirked simultaneously, then she said: "You are a good dude. I like you. I just do not want any more bullshit conversations. I am too intellectually and morally centered for that. And you are, too, most of the time."

He didn't feel bad. He had that coming. He said to Haley, "Can we continue our conversation from the other day?"

"Yes," she replied, "I would like that." Haley slid back in her seat, quietly exhaled, and began: "My husband and I got married right out of high school. We were sweethearts all through high school. We were popular both as individuals and as a couple.

"He played football, ran track, and was in the ROTC. I was a cheerleader, in the honor society, and president of the student council. When we graduated and immediately got married and had a child, it never occurred to us that we would not always be together. After one year together, I decided to go to Chicago State University to become a biology teacher, and he joined the Army. Neither of us saw those choices as being problematic for our future, although I felt some discomfort when we initially talked about those choices."

He leaned forward to take her hands in his, but she pulled back her hands and said: "Not now. Let me talk a little more. Those choices were probably good ones in terms of what each of us wanted and needed, but they were bad choices for the future of our relationship. He spent the next twelve months at Fort Benning in Georgia. After that, he was sent to the Middle East and became a highly decorated soldier.

"After being away for more than nineteen months, he returned home and was stationed again at Fort Benning, which is where he went to Officer Candidate School and became a second lieutenant. For the next four years, I saw him twice for only a few weeks at a time, just long enough for me to have two more children.

"By the time I started to realize what a trap I had allowed myself to be in, it was too late to just hop up and run. I needed a plan and some money to be able to do what I needed to do. So I got a master's degree from the University of Illinois, Chicago; then enrolled in a doctoral program at the University of Chicago; taught for five more years in high school, and then came to the City Colleges of Chicago several years ago. I am still married, technically, but I have not ever lived with my husband for more than a few months at a time since we were married twenty years ago."

Haley paused and reached across the table to take his hands; then she said: "Don't feel sorry for me. I would have liked a situation where my husband was at home in the evening every day; and I could snuggle up in the bed at night and be kissed on a daily basis by the father of my children. But I did not have that, and most days I was okay not having it.

What I was able to have was my freedom to be pretty much in the world in a way that I wanted to be. Again, I have had several lovers over the years, but I never thought I wanted to marry any of them. My mother and father divorced when I was young, but they remarried other people; and I have two sets of parents who now actively serve as two sets of grandparents for my children. So I am now and have been in a good place for some time."

He was happy to hear that Haley was in a good place at this stage in her life, so he said: "If you got divorced, would you ever marry again?"

Haley quickly replied: "Yes. If the right man asked me."

He laughed at that comment because he knew that probably meant that they both would be waiting for a proposal of marriage from the other.

He said to her, "Let's go dancing. There is a set at Cockney Pride just north of here on Wacker Drive. Or we can go south to the El Matador on 75th Street."

Haley said, "Cockney Pride is closer, let's do that."

As they walked towards Cockney Pride, Haley said, "I know how to Bop and Walk, but you have to teach me how to Step."

He smiled and said: "If you can Bop, you can Step."

She replied, "But isn't there is a big difference between the two?"

He responded, "Not really."

Before he had a chance to continue, they were inside of the club, and "I Wanna Sex You Up" by Color Me Badd was playing. He took Haley straight to the dance floor and started to Bop. She followed easily. In the middle of the record, he leaned over and said: "Now relax and dance in the beat rather than to the beat."

Haley heard the words but was not sure she knew what to do. So he pointed to his feet and mouthed: "Just follow me." She made a few mistakes during the rest of the record, but she better understood what she needed to do if she wanted to learn to Step.

After they were seated and with drinks in hand, she said, "So what is the difference between Bopping and Stepping?"

He replied, "As best as I can explain it intellectually, Bopping is a dance routine, whereas Stepping is an art form; although the best Bopping is also an art form and Stepping when you first start out is a dance routine. You can usually tell people who have learned how to Step without first having learned to Bop. These are often young people. The best Steppers, older folks usually, are those who just transitioned from Bopping to Stepping without benefit of formal instruction."

Haley just smiled at his extemporaneous explanation, and then she bluntly told him: "Oops! I am getting a little moist in between my legs. I like bright and articulate men. When I talk with men like you, it is like sexual foreplay without touching physically. In fact, I think it is more intense and exciting than just the physical foreplay—it moves me on so many different levels."

Lisa Stansfield's "All Around The World" came on, and Haley said: "This seems to have a good Bop beat, let me start there and see if I can Step on this up-tempo cut."

As they moved about on the dance floor, he said to himself: '*She's a fast learner. I am going to have to step up my game to keep up with her.*'

As the record stopped, the DJ made a quick transition to Johnny Gill's "My, My, My." Both stopped, turned, and returned to the dance floor. Without talking about it, they quickly slid into the arms of each other and started to Walk. He closed his eyes and kissed her on the ear lightly. She shivered and pulled him closer and said, "Be careful, boy!" He chuckled and pulled her closer.

They both thought that the evening may have musically climaxed with that song until they were almost back to their table and the DJ snuck in Chante Moore's "Love's Taken Over (Quiet Storm Mix)." They both instantly recognized it as a tune to which they could do a variety of dances. They returned to the dance floor. He started deftly with a few Bop moves for a minute or so, then nodded his head and said, "Now," and in slow motion went into Stepping. Tears came to her eyes, and she just said, "Wow." Towards the end of the record, he let her hand go and then grabbed it and pulled her close and started to Walk.

After they had left the noise of the dance club, she asked: "Can I spend the night with you?"

He replied, "Yes, that will be a first for us!"

They both agreed that the evening was fun, and they seemingly rejoiced in it. Both tried not to mess with the flow of the evening, so they hugged and fell silent as they walked to the parking facility where they parked their cars.

He said: "My condo is in Hyde Park. Just follow me. I have two spaces in the garage, so you can take my second space."

She squeezed his hand and said: "Player!"

He replied, "Part-time only."

They both smiled and then laughed heartily at that exchange.

He offered champagne and food after they were settled on the black and white couch facing identically shaped television and hi-fi systems in his condo.

She declined his offer but said, "Quite nice. I like the simplicity of your color scheme and the contours of your furniture. I could live in this space."

He offered: "Would you like to?"

She hesitated and replied, "Yes."

And then she stood up, raised her dress, removed her panties, and sat on his lap facing him. "But first show me how much I would be welcomed in your space," she continued.

He lifted her, held her smooth behind as he walked to the other side of the room with her legs wrapped around his waist, and sat her on top of the hi-fi system. He dropped to his knees, put her legs on his shoulder, and began another act of creation to parallel what he had done on the dance floor. He moaned, she screamed, and then they copulated and fell on the black rug fighting each other in a way that only two lovers who love one another deeply can appreciate—a paradisal encounter.

When they returned to this side of consciousness, he was still deep inside of her; and they held each other tightly and tried to meld their bodies. And for a fleeting second, it felt as if they had accomplished that impossible feat. She said, "Please don't move." And they both went home again after being in that rapturous embrace for only a few minutes.

When they awoke the next morning in his bed, he told Haley that she needed to call her mother and tell her where she was. After Haley had hung up the phone after talking with her mother, he walked into the bedroom with breakfast on a tray with four short legs. As he approached the bed, he suggested that she sit up so that he could place the tray across her legs. He had prepared slices of turkey bacon, toasted cinnamon-raisin English muffins, fresh fruit of various kinds, Starbucks' decaf coffee (to which he had added Häagen-Dazs vanilla ice cream and some coffee supplement), and strawberry preserves from France.

He said, "You can start eating. I am going to get my food."

Haley could only smile as she watched him exit the bedroom.

When he returned, he turned on the television set in the bedroom, climbed into bed next to her, kissed her gently, bit into a piece of bacon, and said to her: "I have recordings of 'Oprah.' Would you like to watch that for a few minutes?"

Haley said, "Yes. I like Oprah."

As they sat in bed and ate breakfast and watched "Oprah," he thought to himself, '*I am so comfortable here with Haley. More comfortable than I have been in a long, long time.*' Just then his new flip cellular phone rang. It was Nicole.

He and Nicole had occasionally talked, but neither had spoken directly to April after that night in the club when April abruptly left without saying goodbye. Nicole said she occasionally heard about April at the hospital, but she had no direct contact with her.

Nicole said, "April passed yesterday. The funeral is at Bond Chapel on the University of Chicago campus on Saturday at 1:00 P.M. I'll see you then. Goodbye."

He was completely devastated and started to blubber. He stopped when Haley placed her hand on his arm and said, "April is dead."

His arm reflexively moved fairly high off the bed even with the weight of Haley's hand on it. He stared at Haley and finally said: "How do you know that?" He loudly repeated: "How do you know that?"

Haley pulled him into her breast and said: "You never understood how and why we found each other so easily after Nicole left you? Did you?"

Justin found himself speechless. He tried to utter words, but only sounds emanated from his lips.

Haley said, "I will go with you to the funeral if you don't mind."

Haley held him for a few more minutes, got out of the bed after gently placing his head on a wet pillow, took her tray to the kitchen, came back to the bedroom, and then carried his tray to the kitchen. Even in that moment of deep despair, he glanced furtively at Haley's behind through eyes made cloudy by the gush of tears from the news about April. He exhaled quietly and made an entreaty to Haley to tell him more when she returned to the bed with more coffee for both of them.

Haley started, "As you probably have guessed, April and I know one another. She is my first cousin on my mother's side. I am not from Antigua, but my mother is. April is the daughter of my mother's youngest sister. April and I met a couple of years ago at the University of Chicago because we are both in The Division of Biological Sciences at the University and had a shared interest in identifying a rare disease and finding a cure for it.

"My interest in biology centers on that disease that killed Scottie and now April. It will also kill my mother and perhaps me if no cure is found for it. Over the past several years, we have been able to identify and name the disease. We also think we know the etiology of the disease. We do not yet have a cure or treatment for the disease."

He sat in the bed with Haley and stared at the television. It all made sense to him now. He had a source for both his comfort and discomfort with Haley. He reached for Haley because he now thought she needed as much comfort as he did.

Haley said, "I am okay. Let me hold you."

With that, she laid on his right side for a few minutes just holding his hand. She kissed him on the lips lightly, threw her right leg over his lower body, and went to sleep. He tried to keep his eyes open and watch television, but the comfort of Haley's body and smooth skin took him where he did not want to go but needed to go. They both slept in their respective positions for two hours.

The ringing of the phone woke them. It was Haley's mother. He had suggested to Haley that she give his cellular phone and home phone numbers to her mother in case she needed to find Haley. He handed Haley the phone and went to the bathroom off the kitchen rather than in the bedroom.

He was fixing a knack for them when Haley came from the bedroom, took his hand, and said: "My husband is in town. I have to go, but I will talk with you later today and join you on Saturday for April's services. I am not surprised that he just showed up without any notice to me about what he was doing. Now you have a better sense of what he is about as a man."

He did not respond to her comments except to nod his head slightly.

He walked with her to the garage, less for her safety and more for him to be able to spend a little more time with her. They embraced and kissed as he helped her into her car. As she drove in front of him to leave the garage, she pressed her index finger to her lips and then turned it to him in a gesture that made him both happy and sad. He returned the gesture, but he wasn't sure that she saw it. It was such a poignant gesture coming from her in that moment. He waved at one of the maintenance guys who always seemed to be in the garage no matter the time of day or whether he was coming in or leaving the building. He exhaled and returned to his condo.

He became tearful as he sat in a room off of the kitchen drinking a glass of juice. He wasn't sure whether the tears were because of Haley leaving him for a while or April leaving him forever, or both. What he was sure of was that he wanted to have another year, month, week, day, hour, minute, or even second with April. He missed her so much that for a moment he thought about joining her. That thought was quickly followed by Haley's conversation about knowing April, and the previous thought quickly went away.

CHAPTER EIGHTEEN

Paean to Life

He had asked Nicole and Haley to meet him in Ida Noyes Hall down the street from Bond Chapel so that they could walk together to the services for April. He saw Nicole and Haley sitting and talking as he entered the social room on the east side of the building. He thought to himself, *'Wow! Why do men always have to make choices about women in this society?'* Both women were dressed in black with hats that dramatically framed their gorgeous faces but somehow did not diminish the solemn occasion or appear to be inappropriate as is sometimes the case with similar attire and under similar circumstances.

They both rose to greet him, they kissed and hugged in pairs, and then they did a group hug that was longer and more sensuous than any one of them probably intended, given the event they were about to attend. They all seemed to have wanted that and seemed to have quickly dismissed any thoughts of impropriety.

With him in the middle, they joined hands and walked to the west side of Ida Noyes Hall. There they descended a flight of stairs, crossed Woodlawn Avenue, walked west around the south end of Rockefeller Chapel, snaked through the campus sidewalks and the Harper Quadrangle, and stopped as they stood at the east entrance of Bond Chapel off the quadrangle. No one said a word, but it was obvious that they were all taking in the resplendence of the chapel.

He had visited both Bond and Rockefeller chapels, and in some ways felt that Bond Chapel paled in comparison to its huge brother to the east, Rockefeller Chapel. Rockefeller Chapel is a towering structure and holds 1700 people compared to the 150 people Bond Chapel holds.

However, he knew that is what April would have wanted—an intimate setting with close friends in a sunlit environment greatly enhanced by the warmth of light coming through beautiful stained-glass windows. The three of them held hands as they stood looking down at April in the shiny, dark-mahogany coffin. Not even death was able to come close to entirely diminishing April's beauty.

As if on signal, they all quietly wept and held one another's hand even tighter. As they turned to offer condolences to Alfred, April's husband, he gestured for all of them to sit next to him in the front row near the coffin. They dutifully sat and continued to hold hands. It appeared that Alfred was broken by April's passing, and Justin wondered whether or not he would survive to take care of his children, "creolized" even more than April by his input.

Justin thought that the service for April was relatively short, forty minutes at the most. At the end of the eulogy, the Episcopal clergyman had an assistant announce that a repast would be held down the street at Ida Noyes Hall immediately following the service.

"This time," Justin told them, "let's just go down 59th street to get to Ida Noyes Hall. We won't have to walk through the campus."

He walked with Haley and held hands while Nicole and Alfred walked together and held hands. He thought to himself, '*That would be interesting if Alfred and Nicole wound up together.*' He quickly remembered that Nicole was happily married to a "brother," so he quickly dismissed that thought.

As he entered the building that they had left not too long ago, someone tapped him on the shoulder. He turned to his right and saw his old friend Sarah. They embraced and pecked each other on the cheek. Haley seemed to instinctively know what the situation was and waited to be introduced.

Justin said to Haley, "Haley this is an old friend, Sarah. Sarah this is a new friend, Haley."

To Sarah, Justin said, "Come and join us."

She replied, "Thanks. I would like that."

The three of them joined Nicole, Alfred, and April's two children and other relatives at a large round table in the center of the room on the south end of the building. Justin wondered if he should say something to Alfred in private. Before he could make a decision about that, someone tapped him on the shoulder. Before he could fully turn to see who was trying to get his attention, he saw part of a blue Air Force uniform out of the corner of his left eye. Immediately he said to himself, '*Oh shit! Haley's husband.*'

He rose, stood looking in the eyes of Haley's husband, extended his hand, and said: "Hi, I am Justin Frambo."

Haley's husband shook his hand and replied: "Yes. I know who you are. Haley told me about you. I am General Powell. Can we talk outside?"

Justin said, "I would prefer that we just went to one of the study rooms in the basement here and talked." Justin pointed to the door just north of where they stood, "It's this way."

Both men walked to the door, went down a flight of stairs, and entered an unoccupied room where they sat across from one another at an old round table.

General Powell said, "I am here to take my wife back by any means necessary."

Justin smiled at those words and replied, "And I intend to keep her by any means necessary."

At that, they both were out of their seats and tussling. Within seconds, Justin had lifted the general off the floor and thrown him on the ground on his back. That move surprised him and probably the general because the general was much larger than Justin: six inches taller and sixty pounds heavier. They glared at each other for a second, and then the general got up and walked out of the room.

Justin recognized that a burst of adrenaline had allowed him to best the general, but he wished that confrontation had never taken place. He understood that the general did not want Haley and just wanted to show the world that he could take her back under his control, which is why he did not try to extend the confrontation between him and the general.

He sat again at the table and thought back about how in the span of a few hours, he had experienced so many emotions: deep sorrow at losing April; joy at being with Haley, Nicole, and Sarah; pathos for Alfred and his loss; wonder at April's children under trying circumstances; fear when the general walked in; anger when he sat across the table from the general; and amazement when he realized that he put the general on his back on the floor.

He had not heard her come in, but he suddenly realized that Haley was standing at his side. She took the chair opposite him where her husband had been seated just a short time ago.

With a wry smile on her face, she said: "You are either a silver-tongued fox or a wily fool."

He replied: "Or both. Let's just say lucky. Did he say anything to you when he left?"

Haley replied, "Yes. He said he would see me at home."

Justin asked: "How does this end?"

Haley replied, "I honestly don't know. I do know that I am not going to get the short end of the stick."

He now had a wry smile as he thought about how much confidence she had as she made that pronouncement. He thought to himself, '*Sho' you right!*

In spite of the solemnity of the occasion, no one seemed inclined to want to leave the gathering. So Nicole suggested that they all go to a newly opened French Restaurant near 55th Street and Lake Park Avenue. Everyone nodded to indicate his or her agreement. April would be cremated, but that would not take place until the following week.

Alfred gave instructions to the funeral director, and they all piled into two limousines to go to the restaurant, which was only about three-quarters of a mile northeast of the chapel. The restaurant was crowded, but they were readily accommodated because Nicole was the friend of a woman who was the owner and chef.

The food at the restaurant exceeded everyone's expectations, and the opportunity for him to be with Nicole, Haley, and Sarah at the same time sent Justin to a place that he wished he could remain forever. As he watched the conversations around the table, including the one Alfred was having with his kids, he noticed that the heaviness of the day started to lift, and joy reigned again in the group. He started to feel that Alfred would survive and find someone to give him close to what he got from April.

When they finished eating, Nicole announced that her husband was coming to get the kids to take them with her children to the Windermere Hotel just a few blocks east of the restaurant. He was bringing two nannies to keep all of the kids so that the adults could have an evening out on the town. She paused for a moment and concluded: "That is what April would have wanted. A celebration of her life." To which all heads nodded in agreement. Nicole further added, "We will start down the street at the Checkerboard Lounge in Harper's Court and listen to some blues, then to the jazz club near there to hear some more uplifting sounds, then to the High Chaparral to dance, and end the evening with breakfast at Mellow Yellow."

Haley leaned over and whispered to Justin: "You know I am coming with you."

To which he replied, "But what about the general?"

Haley laughed and said: "He can keep the kids for one night given all of the nights I have kept them. And if he doesn't want to do that, my mother will stay at the house with them. This is for April, me, and you. The general doesn't count in this moment." She kissed him on the cheek and whispered: "That was for April, me, Sarah, and Nicole."

He choked a bit and looked around the table to see who had been looking. Everyone saw Haley kiss him, but only Nicole grimaced at the sight. But then she smiled broadly as if she had some recollections of good times she had spent with Justin.

Nicole's husband, Donald, walked in shortly after they had started to eat. All of the children and nannies sat at a table right next to theirs. Nicole had ordered for Donald and her children, so their food was brought out a few minutes after their arrival. When they had finished the meal, Justin beckoned the waiter for the check by getting his attention and using his right hand to imitate writing of something in the open palm of his left hand.

They had not talked about how payment for the meal would be handled, but no one feigned paying after Justin got the check for the food. He was happy about that because he did not like that game and he wanted very much to make the gesture solely for April and solely by himself. He felt good, and he knew that Haley felt that.

She said, "You know I would have shared that expense with you, but I got that you wanted to do that alone. If you need some money, let me know. I have on me eight hundred dollars in cash and two credit cards with a limit of thirty thousand dollars each. You can get all of that."

He smiled because he knew that she meant exactly what she said, and his feelings for her could only be expressed at the moment by them touching their thumbs and index fingers together to form a diamond, a metaphor for so many aspects of their relationship.

After the kids had left to go to the hotel with the nannies, Nicole suggested that they walk the two and a half blocks to the Checkerboard Lounge. Justin and Haley held hands; Nicole and her husband, Donald, held hands; and Alfred and Sarah held hands. Justin thought to himself, *'The universe does have an order that we will never understand! April is still here with us.'*

Outside of the Checkerboard, there was an enormous crowd because Muddy Waters was appearing that evening. For some reason, they were ushered to the front of the line and immediately seated in a reserved section of the club.

Muddy Waters was on the stage singing, and there was a buzz in the air that he had never felt before. After Muddy Waters had finished singing "Got My Mojo Working," he went right into "Baby Please Don't Go." After only a few minutes into the song, ten White dudes and a couple of White ladies came into the club and took reserved seats at tables that were close to the stage and in the center of the room.

After a few more choruses of the song he was singing, Muddy Waters hollers out to Mick Jagger a few times to come on stage and join him. Mick Jagger hesitates, but after a little coaxing comes up on stage and jumps around and sings with Muddy Waters. After "Baby, Please Don't Go," Muddy Waters goes into the extended version of "Mannish Boy." With Mick Jagger jumping around on stage like a little mannish boy, Muddy Waters and Jagger get a groove that appears to electrify the crowd.

At some point during the song, things get wild when Muddy Waters invites Buddy Guy (who owned the club); Junior Wells; various members of Mick Jagger's band such as Keith Richards and Ronnie Woods; and several other bluesmen in the audience to come on stage and sing and play. Justin thought: *'What a raucous evening! The crowd appears to have gone berserk, and what started out as a jam session became a full-fledged concert by originators and masters of Chicago Blues and a British rock group mostly known and appreciated by Blacks for its hit song, 'Miss You'.'*

By the time the show was over, both audience and performers appeared to be spent. Nicole, however, insisted that they stick to the plan and go to the Vahalla Lounge down on 53rd Street in the Hyde Park Bank Building to listen to some jazz. No one knew who would be appearing there, but as they entered the long narrow room, Gene

Ammons and Dexter Gordon were playing. John Young was playing piano, and Steve McCall was on drums. The tune they were playing was titled "The Happy Blues." When Justin leaned over and whispered the name of the song to the group, a few tears of joy and sorrow could be seen on every face in the group.

Justin ordered more champagne for the group, and they stayed to hear a few more selections. When "Lonesome Lover Blues" started, Alfred quietly left the table and went to the washroom where he remained for about ten minutes. Justin noticed that no one expressed concern because they all apparently knew what that was about. The group did decide to leave after Alfred returned to the table.

Alfred said, "No, we can stay here for a little while longer. I'm ok."

Sarah, who had been silent almost all of the evening, took his hand and said: "We know. We just want to move our bodies in space and continue our celebration of April's life."

Alfred replied, "Great. But you will have to help me with that."

Everyone in the group laughed, but Sarah told him, "Just follow my lead." Again, everyone laughed.

They had the limousines take them to the High Chaparral. When Justin saw the place, he thought how unbelievably diminished it was from its heyday as a place for jazz, blues, and R&B performances. Justin recalled that in its heyday, Chicagoans and out-of-towners could see Harold Melvin and The Blue Notes, The Impressions, Curtis Mayfield, Michael Jackson, Natalie Cole, Chi-Lites, War, Tyrone Davis, Bobby "Blue" Bland, Bobby Womack, Lee Shot Williams, Earth Wind and Fire, Count Basie, Ari Brown, Sonny Stitt, Miles Davis, and other Black entertainers at this venerable show venue on the South Side of Chicago. On any given night, he recalled, you might see celebrities in the audience such as Michael Jordan, Muhammad Ali, Joe Frazier, Scottie Pippen, and Mike Tyson.

From what Justin could observe, this night it was mostly the wannabe pimps, whores, and hustlers who made up most of the crowd. Justin also thought he saw in the mix some South Siders and voyeurs from the North Side, including a White photographer who would later publish his pictures of individuals in various South Side clubs in a best seller. But who cared. "Push It" by Salt N Pepa was playing when the group walked in, and as soon as they had been seated at a table, Sarah grabbed Alfred and took him to the dance floor.

Oddly enough, the boy seemed to have rhythm, which prompted Sarah to say: "Ok. You are doing fine. Don't try to follow me now, just keep feeling the beat and respond to it."

The DJ had not phased out "Push It" before Tone Loc's "Wild Thing" came up. Both Nicole and Haley jumped up to dance on that one. Neither Justin nor Donald could object. The four of them did the wild thing as they moved to the "Wild Thing." Justin felt so alive that he almost got teary eyed.

Rick James' "Give It To Me Baby" came up next. Donald and Nicole got even wilder on that one, but neither Haley nor Justin ever liked that cut. So they waved at Donald and Nicole and sat down. Sarah and Alfred sat quietly at the table talking about god knows what, but they were both smiling and touching hands. Justin said to himself, '*Y'all go for it.*'

They continued to dance for another hour or so, and just when everyone seemed ready to leave to go to breakfast at Mellow Yellow, the extended version of "Rapture" by Blondie came up. All of the women rushed to the floor ahead of the men and made moves that Justin believed none of the men had seen before.

He thought to himself, '*What a way to end the evening.*'

The men were dancing, but their real inclination appeared to be to watch the women dance and laugh: Nicole spinning and moving her body as graceful as a ballet dancer; Haley prancing and dropping down like he had never seen her; Sarah was moving fast to the music but was gliding as she did so. The men all stopped dancing and just watched the ladies. It was breathtaking to see three beautiful women in their own zone in their own style dance through the long version of "Rapture," nearly 10 minutes in length. Wow!

They had already decided to leave after "Rapture" ended, but the disc jockey put "Before I Let Go" by Maze and Frankie Beverly on the turntable.

Sarah said to Alfred, "This is a good record to learn how to Bop and move into Stepping." In the spirit of the evening, all three couples returned to the dance floor as sort of a final toast to April. Alfred still appeared to be sad, but Justin could tell that he was feeling better because he smiled on several occasions when Sarah did a double spin as he turned her around and he could see her lovely legs gliding across the floor. "The Look In Your Eyes" came up next, and Alfred and Sarah stayed on the floor while everyone else sat.

For a minute, it seemed as if Alfred had both learned to Bop and Step all in one evening, at least enough to keep up with Sarah. It felt as if April was out there helping Alfred. You could tell that Sarah felt that and was rocking to it! After that song, they all returned to the table and stood and held hands and bowed their heads in a gesture to April.

Then they raised their nearly empty champagne glasses and said in unison: "To April."

The DJ saw that and dropped Larry Graham's "One In A Million You" on the turntable. Without words, all three couples returned to the dance floor. And that is how that part of the evening ended.

When they got to Mellow Yellow at 4:00 A.M. in the morning, they all appeared to be surprised to find that there was still a crowd waiting to be seated. As they talked about whether or not they wanted to stay and wait, the person at the hostess stand left her position and came to where they stood and beckoned for them to follow her. They all expressed surprised and seemed grateful. As they reached the table to sit down, Justin surreptitiously handed the hostess a twenty-dollar bill. With barely a nod, the hostess acknowledged and thanked him.

After such a long and trying day, everyone in the group appeared to be surprisingly alert and chirpy. The chatter around the table was energizing, and Alfred appeared to be grateful to be surrounded by friends who seemingly loved April and him. Justin thought that Alfred was tired and was settling into a comfort zone that would lead to sleep, but Alfred managed to stay in the moment and be engaged with the group.

After almost two hours of banter and good food, Haley said, "You all can come and rest with me and Justin in a condo around the corner from here if you like." Justin smiled at that and nodded in agreement.

Everyone looked around the table for a consensus, and Alfred said, "Let's go."

Later that same day, Nicole, Donald, and Alfred went to the Windermere Hotel to get the kids and take them back to the sanctity of the suburbs. Alfred and Sarah exchanged telephone numbers and embraced like forlorn lovers. Haley checked in with her mother and was told that the general had left town without saying goodbye. Haley told Justin about that, and she also told him that that news saddened her for a few seconds. She also told him that she understood that it was probably best for all concerned for that to have happened.

Haley said to Justin, "Let's go see a movie."

He replied, "How about the 'The Empire Strikes Back' the new 'Star Wars' movie."

Haley said, "Fine."

They decide to stay in the neighborhood and walk around the corner to the Hyde Park Theater, seemingly always struggling to stay open. The movie was entertaining, and the popcorn was delicious. They decided to eat dinner at Medici, but that was a distance farther than they wanted to walk. So they hailed a cab that took them to 57th Street and Harper Avenue near the METRA station.

The hostess greeted them with a smile and offered them an intimate booth near the rear of the restaurant.

Haley immediately and gently took both of his hands and said, "You know the journey must begin again."

He puckered his lips and replied, "Yes. For both of us. How do we start again?"

Haley did not immediately respond but finally said: "I am going to have to return to my husband at some point. You will have to find a wife who will complement you intellectually but not necessarily emotionally. That will work for both of you for a long time, but it will not end well. I know this conversation is a downer for you, but it is also a bummer for me, too. I love you more than you will ever know."

She came and sat next to him and laid her head on his shoulder. They stayed in that position for a full hour, with only a break for them to eat the pizza and drink the beer they had ordered. After he had paid the check, they took a cab back to his condo. Haley decided that it was better if she went directly to her car in the garage rather than return to the comfort of his condo.

In her rear-view mirror, she watched him standing in the middle of the garage quietly crying and not moving. Her inclination was to turn the car around and return to his condo and his bed, but she decided otherwise and kept the car moving out of the garage and onto the street going north. When she got to 49th Street, she had to pull over and let her tears go where they needed to go.

CHAPTER NINETEEN

Moments

As he sat at the table with Charlotte and Jackie after dancing with the two of them together, he wondered if he should get the telephone number of Jackie or Charlotte for future use, but he decided not to try to make more of the moment. That was hard for him—not to try to make more of a moment that he enjoyed. Experience had taught him, however, that to pursue moments beyond a certain point often led to untoward consequences—often for no other reason than the fact that those moments were not meant to be any more than that.

That thought immediately made him think about his second wife, Gloria, and the chance meeting they had in the garage of the building in which they both once lived. He remembered how his second wife had been standing in the garage at the same moment Haley had left him. She had asked one of the maintenance men standing in the garage at that time to introduce her to him.

That was one of those moments that he should have just let be an enjoyable moment. Instead, on a cold, blustery winter day in Chicago more than two decades ago, he decided to pursue a young woman more than twenty years his junior. It was not just him being a dirty old man. He had seen her before but had ignored her because of her age. Now he stood before her staring into her eyes, one of which was slightly bigger than the other.

She wore a gray man's hat with the brim turned down all the way around and a long, gray overcoat that almost covered her feet. She was young and handsome, and the sight of her up close made his heart skip a beat. This same woman, officially a wife now, had put him out that past winter, or rather he had made the choice to leave when she asked for a divorce after seven years of courtship, eighteen years of marriage, four children, a huge mortgage, and a mountain of feelings he found both challenging to understand and describe.

He heard the words she said as she told him why she wanted a divorce, but he never really understood the reason she wanted a divorce. He suspected that the real reason was that while he idolized her because of her intellect, he never really adored her in a way that she wanted to be adored—that adoration or rapturous love that you see on television and in the movies.

The relationship with her was the longest and most contestable of any relationship he had been in, and for that, in many ways, he was grateful. They had had both the time and the energy to develop a relationship that, even when it was difficult, helped them both forge a view of the world that they both knew would take them through life under the best and most difficult circumstances.

So as she put it, "The divorce was needed in order to save the relationship." He didn't like admitting it, but he knew there was a bit of truth in what she said.

At their meeting in the garage, they had exchanged numbers and promised to be in contact with one another soon. On the following evening, he called and invited her to go to dinner at a local restaurant in the Hyde Park neighborhood where they both lived. The restaurant, Orly's, was located on the corner of 55th Street and Hyde Park Boulevard.

He had always thought that the latter was an intriguing street because it is one of only a few streets in Chicago that runs in two different directions—east-west and north-south. Now, he thought, it was even more intriguing and well-known because it is the east-west access street to the home of the newly elected president, Barack Obama, and the president's home can be easily viewed from this street.

He had always had mixed feelings about Orly's, and he wasn't sure why. The food, overall, was good at Orly's. The atmosphere was interesting—you entered the restaurant directly into a bar with just six or seven seats; behind that was a long room with two levels of seating; and behind that was another single-level seating area. The lighting and atmosphere in the place were gothic, in some ways reminiscent of many of the buildings and rooms at the nearby University of Chicago.

They had opted to walk to Orly's from the high-rise building in which they lived primarily because parking was always an issue in the neighborhood. As they had anticipated and talked about, it was cold that evening; and they knew that in Chicago in January, that is what you get: a coldness that is sometimes exacerbated by a variety of factors—wind, proximity to the lake, area of the city, number of high-rise buildings in an area, and so on.

The restaurant was not far, however, especially if they cut through the parking lot of the Jewish synagogue and school that was just south of their building. When he saw her for the second time, that evening at dinner, he realized that she had an easy charm that he liked. They initially talked about how they had seen each other in the garage and never spoke though each had been inclined to do so. They had acknowledged each other with eye contact and a head nod, but no words were ever exchanged. They both smiled at that bit of reality and then got off into a conversation about the kinds of cars they drove.

She drove a silver, four-door Pontiac that was several years old. She told him that choice had been made based upon her pocketbook and job. He drove a Mazda RX 7, a choice based mostly on the car's design—its engine and body.

At some point, the conversation over dinner went into some sophomoric exchange about the meaning of life. Neither seemed inclined to elevate the conversation for fear of scaring off the other, but it was clear to each of them that they had met their match—on several different levels. They did not want to end the evening, so they went back to the building where they lived—to his apartment. She told him later that she thought she would never see him again, although she wanted to; so she made the decision to do what she had never done before: have a one-night stand.

The one-night stand lasted for twenty-five years, a quarter of a century. Sitting now in his newly acquired apartment on Clark Street in the South Loop, he thought about how they had managed to be together for so long given so many differences between them, not the least of which was age. When she had first seriously asked him for a divorce in a counseling session that had been initiated in relationship to their oldest son, who had been diagnosed with ADHD, he was stunned.

The counselor had made a query about something, and then posed the question to him: "Do you love her as much as you did when you first met her?"

His quick and spontaneous answer was, "Yes. Even more."

And Gloria immediately followed with, "Enough to give me a divorce?"

He just said, "Yes."

Somehow the setting they were in seemed appropriate for this life-altering conversation. All that was missing was a little food and a few drinks. The therapist held her therapy sessions in the basement of an apartment building where she lived. It was a French basement where you could see out of the windows although it was a late-evening, wintery day when they were there, and the heavy snows of Chicago covered the bottom of the windows with dirty, white stuff. There was jazz playing in the background, Thelonious Monk, a hint of incense in the air, and curiously low lighting of various hues.

Because the therapist had a master's degree in social work from the University of Chicago, his inclination was to stay in the moment and be responsive and respectful. He had received his doctorate from that same institution a few years earlier, and he thought that institution to be one of the finest in the world, although his wife, Gloria, would have argued that Northwestern University (where she had gone to grad school) held that honor and position.

Although he had agreed to attend the therapy session that evening and other times, he did not believe that therapy of any kind could help anyone. As a young man, he had gone to a community service center to receive therapy after several unsettling incidents in his life had him reeling from life's blows to his young psyche. He went to five or six counseling sessions, but he never saw any of the sessions as being useful. So he stopped going.

CHAPTER TWENTY

Losing Love

He was sorry that he was getting a divorce from his wife and children. He and this wife, the second one, had been in each other's life for more than a quarter of a century—half of her life and almost a third of his. Although they had talked about a divorce in the counseling session almost a year before, it was not until September of 2008 that she walked into the kitchen while he was cooking and told him that she had obtained the services of an attorney to file for a divorce. He was immobilized as he stood there hating her and what she had told him.

He finally said, "Ok."

Then he took off the apron he wore, turned the oven and stovetop burners off, and walked down the stairs and out of the house.

Initially, he walked out of the house just to get some fresh air and clear his head a bit. He also knew that he was so angry that if he did not leave, he might be inclined to hurt Gloria. He was glad that he walked out of the house, and he got in his BMW and headed down State Street to Macy's.

He normally would have gone to the 2nd floor at Macy's where the men's clothes and furnishings could be found. This time he went to the 8th floor where household furnishings were located. As soon as she said that she had the services of an attorney for a divorce, he decided to move out and get his own space. He knew that his own place and furnishings for it would be costly, but he just said to himself, '*Fuck it.*'

While he was hurting at the thought of a divorce, he was almost gleeful at the prospect of again having his own space and furnishing it in a way that he wanted. Before they moved into the house they now occupied together as man and wife; he had lived in Hyde Park in a condominium on a higher floor in the same building as she did. He had decorated the place almost entirely achromatically—black, white, and chrome. To the white walls, black carpet, and black and white couches and chairs; he added futuristic chrome lamps that looked like inverted rocket ships. He had also added black and chrome wall sculptures that somehow made you think of planets in space.

Like many bachelor pads, the entire color scheme centered on the stereo sound system. His was Zenith's Allegro stereo console that was popular during the 70s. The system was white laminated wood that was so aesthetically pleasing and different from other consoles because only the top had right angles. The bottom of the console was curved, and there was a matching television console of the same shape.

He had conceded to Gloria the entire task of decorating the house that they now occupied, mostly because he had had that experience several times and she had never had that experience. Her sense of aesthetics was the opposite of his. She chose to have bold colors all over the place, including the walls at one point. He had lived in that setting with her for more than thirteen years, but it never resonated with him in the same way that his condominium had.

He had bought the condominium in the same year that he changed jobs—from a high school teacher to a college administrator. To help pay for the condominium and keep up his child support commitment for the children he had brought into the world with Betty, for six years straight he taught education, history, and philosophy courses during the summer in the day; and in the late afternoon and evening, he delivered telephone books.

Some members of his family and some friends marveled at his willingness to work so hard and not want to hang in the streets like many of his buddies. For him, it was a way of life. At the age of nine, he had worked in a coal yard carrying coal, wood, oil, and even ice. At the age of ten, he remembered working in a grocery store on the corner of 39th and Wentworth. So working hard for what you wanted out of life was all he had ever known. It was not at all a stretch for him.

When he was a young man, during the summer when all of his buddies were on the basketball court of a Catholic school and church that was about a half block south of the store in which he worked, he carried groceries to the houses of families in the neighborhood.

Occasionally he would sit the basket full of groceries on the ground, put his hands and head on the fence that surrounded the court, and stand and watch the fellows play for four or five minutes. It never occurred to him to not work at the grocery store and play basketball instead on St. Elizabeth's court. Since his family was poor, his focus was on having money to buy the things he wanted and that his parents could not provide.

As he walked through Macy's contemplating what furniture he would buy for an apartment he did not yet have, he decided to sit for a moment on an attractive, red leather couch. That, in and of itself, was interesting because he would have never bought the couch for fear of it being too jarring each time that he saw it. But somehow the red couch became the symbolic axis for the rotation of some powerful memories from his past that were related to his efforts to be comfortable in the face of a pending divorce.

His stay in Macy's on the red leather couch had turned into several hours of him recalling how he had arrived at this point in his life where he was contemplating what furniture he would buy for an apartment he did not yet have and not a lot of money for either. He thought again about how Haley had left him standing in the garage crying, and how as soon as he turned to go back to his condo, he saw his present wife standing in the garage talking to one of the maintenance men who introduced them to each other. That wife, Gloria, was a lovely woman who had taken him at a low point in his life and brought contentment to his soul again.

They had had a tumultuous relationship in the beginning; but for reasons neither could ever explain, they remained in each other's life for almost a quarter of a century. They often made love madly, traveled to the Caribbean and other places frequently with and without the four kids they brought into the world, partied like it was 1999, pursued graduate degrees (she three masters, him a Ph.D.), and waxed and waned in their love for one another. But there had been signs all along that the relationship was not a wholesome one.

The first week that they met, they had a heated argument seemingly over nothing of real importance. The argument had started in front of the building where they both lived and got totally out of control within a few short minutes. She had swung at him and missed. At that point, he walked away and entered the garage to get his car and drive off to some unknown destination. When he drove out of the garage, she was blocking his exit to the street. He blew his horn and revved the car's motor. That scared her, and she jumped to the side.

As he drove in front of her, she screamed obscenities at him and threw a glass soda bottle at the car, which broke upon impact and left a small dent in the right fender of the car. He stopped the car to examine the damage but decided not to respond to the assault. They did not speak for several weeks until she called him at work. They went to dinner that evening and made up, but that left a fissure in the relationship that would widen as the years went by.

After seven years of courtship that can only be described as "good times" (an average of great times and heart-breaking moments), they had decided to get married in the islands. She wanted the American Virgin Islands as a setting for the wedding but deferred to his wish for Antigua. He wasn't sure what he would find in making that choice, so he called Haley to talk about it.

She told him that she and her husband had gotten back together and were planning to move to Las Vegas after he retired in a year or so. She had had another child, and her four older kids were all in college. Her father had passed after a long and debilitating disease, and her mother was living with her.

Then she had told him: "What you need won't be found in Antigua. It is here with me, and I have already given it to you. You just have to continue your journey. Find your next wife, finish your doctorate, and write your books. I miss you, and I love you even more now than I ever did."

He heard a deep sob, and the telephone emitted a sound signaling the end of the conversation.

He heard a small bell ring and was startled to find himself at home and not back on the red couch in Macy's. He thought to himself, '*Life has a way of taking you in directions that you neither planned for nor even thought about. Retrospectively, however, it all makes sense because you always seem to be where you need or want to be (or both), and the route taken is the only one that could have gotten you to where you were at a point in time.*'

Those are the thoughts he had as he sat alone in his condo that evening drinking Kahlua and cream over ice. He had ordered Chinese food from the House of Eng located in the Del Prado Hotel not far from his place. He ate there often because the restaurant was situated on the top of the hotel and offered panoramic views of the east side of the city and downtown area. It was one of those places to be in Chicago in the summer. This evening he ordered shrimp egg foo young and beef chop suey.

As he ate, he had both the television on with the audio on mute and Miles Davis on the stereo. He was melancholic, but he had no idea of the source of that feeling. For a second or two, he thought Miles' *Sketches of Spain* playing in the background might have brought on his melancholy. But that wasn't it. That was one of his favorite albums by Miles Davis, and hearing it always brought him great and intense happiness. After an hour or so in that funk, he was able to focus on what Haley had said about continuing his journey. He then called Gloria to tell her that the Virgin Islands would be okay for their wedding.

He then got in his car and drove down 51st Street to Woodlawn Avenue. There he made a left and headed south on Woodlawn Avenue to Rockefeller Chapel. He sat in his car for ten minutes looking at the huge church and thought about the day he would walk through that edifice to receive his doctorate. After that first time, he would make it a point to drive by Rockefeller Chapel at least once a month as a way of being motivated to continue his work on his Ph.D.

He and Gloria had been married in the Virgin Islands that summer and four weeks later had a fabulous reception at the Hyatt Regency on Wacker Drive. They showed pictures of the wedding in the islands on two huge screens in the room, and even he had to admit that there was a fairytale aura to the evening. The evening was almost marred by the no-show status of the photographer who had been paid in advance to capture the evening for future reference, but several friends had brought professional cameras to the occasion and caught it all on film.

Their life together over the next two decades would have its regrets, but overall it was good. They had brought four children into the world, housed and fed them well, and sent them to the Lab School at the University of Chicago. They had finished advanced degrees, bought a nice house in a tony neighborhood in the South Loop in Chicago, and spent time with friends and neighbors that could be described as happy times. Now it was all coming to an end, but he had already been told that his marriage would not end well. He did sometimes wonder if that bit of information had contributed to the end of the marriage or merely foretold its demise.

CHAPTER TWENTY-ONE

Justin's Angels

After his wife had announced her intentions to get a divorce, for the next couple of months, he looked for an apartment in the South Loop, mostly because he was always fond of being in a neighborhood that was predicted by many to be the area to live in during the next half-century or more. He also liked the area because of its proximity to the downtown area, lake, and world-class museums that sat on the lakefront. He liked all of the luxury apartments and condominiums he saw on Michigan Avenue south of Roosevelt Road, but he decided to look at several new buildings north of Roosevelt Road on Clark Street.

The one he finally chose was one on Clark Street that had a 270-degree view of the city. To the west, he could see the administration building of the University of Illinois, Chicago. When he looked north, he could see Sears Tower and other iconic buildings of the downtown area. To the east, he could see the lake and the museum campus with its neoclassical structures and gleaming marble edifices. To the south, he could see parts of McCormick Place, an exhibition and convention center that had burned to the ground and had been rebuilt and extended so that it was now the largest center of its kind in North America.

He moved into his new apartment on south Clark Street on Thanksgiving Day after an enjoyable meal and family gathering that was like many memorable ones that he and Gloria had shared over the years.

It was late in the evening, and as he stood at the bottom of the stairs looking up at Gloria and the kids, she said: "Do you have to go tonight?"

To which he replied, "Yes. Every minute here after tonight will make it harder to leave."

With that exchange, he got into his BMW and drove to his new apartment, which contained only a mattress and a few clothes. He did not rest well that evening, but he did not have to go to work, so he stayed on the mattress for several hours after he had awakened. He had made the initial move to a new life by moving to the new apartment; he now needed to jumpstart a new social life. He called his youngest brother and told him that he wanted his player's card back.

His brother laughed and replied, "You will have to earn it."

He chuckled and replied: "I have been off the dating scene for some time, but I know it will be like learning to ride a bicycle again. You don't think about it. You just get on and peddle."

With his brother's hearty laugh still reverberating in his ear at the end of their conversation, he hung up the phone. His brother had briefly mentioned an upcoming midweek party at the Grand Ballroom on 63rd and Cottage. As he thought about what he needed to do to earn his player's card back, his thoughts initially were not about how to behave but rather how to dress.

He had recently bought a gray pinstripe suit designed by Armani. That was an easy choice although he had other designer suits from which to choose. Armani's clothing, even for women, had always resonated with him most because of the choices of material, colors, cut, and balance.

Almost all of his dress shirts were white, mainly because he thought white would show off a tie better than any other color no matter the color of the tie. The tie he chose to go with his outfit was also designed by Armani: an abstract design—deep yellow background, variously shaped splashes of black, and larger splashes of dark red. Just gorgeous.

As he and his brother entered the Grand Ballroom, a Walk record was starting up. He glanced around the room to find a dance partner and his eyes fell on a woman who had her back turned to him. Her back was completely out, and he immediately thought about Melvin Van Peeble's *Sweet Sweetback*.

He walked towards the table where the lone woman sat, leaned down and kissed her on the back, stood up and waited to be either slapped or cussed out. The woman did neither.

She turned to him and said, "Does that mean you want to dance with me or make love to me?"

He replied, "Both. I don't like either-or propositions."

He then held out his hand to help her rise from the chair.

As they danced around the room on the outer edge of the floor, the woman introduced herself as Rachel. He introduced himself and told her to lean in a bit more so he could better guide her body. He said to himself, '*And to guide your mind.*' The DJ was spot-on that evening. He played several Walk records in secession: "Night and Day" by the Temptations and "Look At Me I'm in Love" by the Moments. The DJ followed those up with "I Could Have Loved You" by the Moments and "Pay Back Is A Dog" by the Stylistics.

Rachel was the best dancer he had ever known. She never missed a step even when he did. In six-inch stiletto hills, she was almost as tall as he was, so she fit easily into his arms, and because she had complied with his request to lean in on his body, they looked as if they were floating around the dance floor.

When they returned to the table where Rachel had been sitting, a woman he had not seen earlier was sitting there. With his help, Rachel quickly sat down; and she immediately introduced the woman to him by saying, "Naima this is Justin. Justin this is Naima."

He took Naima's hand, bowed, and said to himself: '*You made your move too soon.*'

Naima somehow reminded him of April, except she was bigger, taller, and lighter than April. He took drink orders from the two women and headed to the bar.

As he stood at the bar ordering a bottle of champagne, his brother tapped him on the shoulder and said: "Who are those ladies?"

He replied, "Just two ladies that I met tonight."

He told his brother about how he had kissed the shorter, darker one on the back, and how she had responded, to which they both laughed and slapped hands. He then told his brother that he had gotten the telephone number of that same lady, but he thought that might now be a mistake. The other one now mesmerized him.

His brother asked why he had not gotten the other lady's telephone number, and he replied, "Apparently she was in the washroom or dancing when I first walked in. I did not see her until about four dances later. By then I was enjoying the first lady I met. Her name is Rachel.

When I brought Rachel back to the table, the other lady, Naima, was sitting there."

His brother said, "Don't worry, I will take whichever one you don't want. Or maybe you want both of them." That was exactly what he had been thinking.

He did not want to appear to be a jerk, so he decided to call Rachel and ask her to go to dinner with him. She did not answer. He left a message, but he did not get a call back from Rachel. Several weeks passed, and he ran into Rachel and Naima at a Halloween party in the basement of a mutual friend's home. He and his brother watched the bevy of beautiful woman parade before them as the crowd Bopped, Stepped, Walked, and "freestyled" to the music of Willie Hutch, The Whispers, O'Jays, Barry White, Earth Wind and Fire, Denise Williams, Donnie Hathaway, The Delfonics, and other soul groups.

He spoke to both Rachel and Naima, but he did not want to have an extended conversation with either, although he wanted very much to be in the company of Naima. As they usually did whenever they were out together, he and his brother headed their separate ways. Both knew they would touch base several times during the evening, so they were not inclined to be constantly together in any setting. The party was a BYOB one, and Justin had brought four bottles of cheap champagne, actually decently priced champagne, since he avoided the cheap brands.

As he consciously avoided Rachel and Naima that evening, he did a little people watching. At one point, he noticed an acquaintance from the circle that he ran in dancing with a cute and voluptuous young woman. The gentleman was one of the best dancers in the room, and the woman was able to keep up with him for every move he made. Their movements, slight kicks of the feet, and twisting and turning were more aesthetically pleasing than any ballroom dancing he had ever seen. To boot, she was smooth in her footwork and as subtle as a salad dressing that allowed you only to know that it was there but never to make itself what you tasted most.

Several records later, he decided to ask that same woman to dance with him. Initially intimidated by her moves, he decided not to try to outdo her. Instead of dancing to the beat to match her footwork, he decided to dance in the beat. To do that, he knew that his moves could not be at the conscious level of hearing and responding to the beat.

He knew he would have to let go and let his body just follow the beat and bypass the usual processing by the mind. At some point in their creative evolution, he thought, that is probably how most great athletes, musicians, scientists, and artists of various kinds work their magic. In fact, that may be a description of most great acts of creativity.

At the end of the record, the woman introduced herself as Shelby. He responded by saying, "That's a cute name." Without any more conversation, he was Walking with Shelby on a tune by the Temptations called "Heavenly," which made him think to himself: '*How apropos!*' Even Before the record had ended, he had a sense of being carefully scrutinized by someone in the crowd. After he had taken Shelby back to her seat, he looked around the room for his brother and to see who might be watching him. He saw no one.

As he moved towards his seat, however, he saw Rachel and Naima sitting with another woman not too far from where he was sitting. Naima beckoned for him to come over, and he intrepidly did so. All three ladies wore skirts so short that he could not help but keep their legs as a vocal point as he approached them. Only the unnamed woman showed her draws because of her thin legs and both feet flat on the floor side by side. The other two women sat with legs crossed to expose only their outer thighs. Luscious.

Rachel spoke first and said: "Hi, Justin. You know Naima, and this is our friend Mattie. Come and sit with us."

His inclination was to decline the offer, but he wanted to be near Naima. So he sat down. As soon as he set down, Shelby was standing in front of the group and asking to join them.

Before the ladies in the group could respond, he said: "Please. We would love to have you here."

Surprisingly, not a single person objected, and the rest of the evening was spent drinking, talking, dancing, eating, and having a great time. He was not sure why the group took on a hearty party atmosphere, but he was pleased about how the evening turned out.

The next day he got an early-morning call from Rachel. She wanted to accept an invitation to dinner that he had made several weeks ago.

He said he would take her to dinner that evening, but added: "I want all of the ladies from our group last evening to join us."

Rachel was silent for a moment, but she finally said, "Sure. Sure. That should be fun."

He promised to call her back as soon as he had reservations in a nearby restaurant. He also asked that she contact Naima and Mattie. He said that he would call Shelby.

The restaurant that he chose for their outing was a nice little Indian restaurant in the South Loop. He was not a fan of Indian food, but he had never really had a chance to explore that cuisine in any meaningful or thoughtful way. His thought was, '*Let's make this spicy.*'

When he got to the restaurant, all of the ladies were there looking like angels. At that moment, he decided to give them the moniker of "Justin's Angels." The evening was a continuation of the night before. All of the women seemed to enjoy each other's company, and he almost felt like a voyeur, except he had initiated the gathering, so it was his to enjoy.

At one point in the evening, he proposed a toast: "It is seldom that a man gets to enjoy the company of four beautiful women all by himself. And I am glad that I have been able to have such a moment. I did not think it was possible for a situation like this to happen. The interactions between you four gorgeous and intelligent women tonight make me believe that peace in the world is possible. (The ladies laugh for several minutes.) I am so impressed with the way you look and behave this evening that I would henceforth like to refer to you collectively as "Justin's Angels."

And then someone started to shout, "Group hug. Group hug."

After four hours of good food and good company, the group decided they wanted to run the streets together in the future. So they told Justin he should be the one to decide on the activities of the group, although they would all give input to activities for the group. That was the beginning of their run together, and what a run it was.

CHAPTER TWENTY-TWO

The Art of Loving

He had left Charlotte and Juliet sitting at the table and gotten another drink for him and Charlotte. Juliet had again declined an offer to have a drink. She had again said that she was alone and driving home by herself, so she was just being extra cautious.

He wondered if the information about being alone was just an explanation of why Juliet was not drinking alcohol or was she also trying to give him some information to use to see if he would be tempted. For a moment, he did think about pursuing Juliet in an affair of some kind, but he quickly thought about his Angels and what that might mean for the dynamics of the group. So he got up from the table, bowed gracefully to the ladies, and left after kissing each lady on the cheek.

As he drove home from the reunion, he thought about all of the ladies he ran the streets with. When he first thought about running the streets with the ladies, he did not even think that at some point he would have to make a choice to be with one of them exclusively. For now, he just wanted to have fun. He got his first hint of a problem when he arranged to take the Angels to one of Chicago's premier fundraisers, a gala put on by Indigo Magazine at the Pavilion located at the University of Illinois, Chicago.

It was summer time in Chicago in July, with temperatures in the upper 70's, a soft breeze off of Lake Michigan, and women looking good—barelegged in shorts and flat shoes and skimpy tops. The tickets to the gala were $300.00 a person, but he had managed to get four tickets from a friend who worked for an international corporation. The corporation had purchased ten tables for the affair, and he was fortunate enough to get four of the one hundred tickets given out to various individuals and groups.

When he told the ladies about going to the affair at a dinner he had arranged for them at the Firehouse restaurant, the ladies whooped and hollered as if they had gotten tickets to a Super Bowl Game or something comparable for ladies.

One lady asked how many tickets he had, and he told them he had four tickets. The same lady asked: "Which of us is not going to be able to go?"

To which he replied: "We are all going. I bought a fifth ticket so that we could all go."

The whooping and hollering then became so loud that the restaurant's manager came and stood near the table for a minute.

When he arrived at the affair with two of the ladies, he could see that Chicago's elite had come out for the gala. After food and liquor had been served, there was a performance that evening by Frankie Beverly and Maze that made the ladies deliriously happy. After the performance, some of the tastiest desserts ever made were served in an enclosed area of the concert venue. The variety of music for the dancing part of the evening included Chicago house, blues, rhythm and blues, Jazz, Bop, and Stepping music.

At one point in the evening, he had walked away from the group to get champagne for everyone. As he came back to them with a waiter following him with the champagne and dessert, the women, all in white, indeed made him think of angels. But it was Naima, however, that made him think about goddesses. So he asked her to dance, and the magic began.

He had not had a lot of champagne, but he was now higher than he had been in a long, long time. Shortly after he started to dance with Naima, the other three ladies decided to join them. He was amazed that he could keep up with all four of them almost as well as he could any one of them. That inebriating evening went on for another two hours with all four ladies. One by one, however, the group dwindled down to two—him and Naima.

When they decided to sit for awhile on the stones of a garden at the edge of the large enclosed patio where the event was being held, he realized that the other ladies had disappeared, which was reminiscent of April's disappearing acts.

He said to Naima, "All of the other ladies are gone. You ready to go?" She replied, "Yes."

He dropped her off in an area of South Shore near the South Shore Cultural Center. He saw her to the door, but he did not make any romantic moves. Instead, he hugged her, kissed her lightly on the cheek, and watched her disappear into her apartment. She waved from a third-floor window to signal to him that she was safely in her apartment. He waved back. Then he walked slowly to his car, got in, and drove north to his apartment. He was too tired and inebriated to assess the events of the evening thoroughly, especially in relationship to Naima. But he did think, '*She may be the one.*'

He did not hear from any of the ladies for several days until Shelby called. He thought that was interesting. She needed a date for an affair that was coming up in two weeks—a gathering for an old friend who was celebrating a milestone in her life—50th Birthday. He said yes to her invitation to join her.

When he picked Shelby up a few weeks later, she was stunning in a gray lace dress that was tight and hit her just above her knees. When they got to the party, they each instinctively knew just to mingle as a single, and after a peck on the cheek, they did not see one another for several hours until he noticed her dancing with a well-dressed, handsome fellow on Willie Hutch's "I Can Sho Give You Love."

The fellow Shelby was now dancing with wasn't as smooth as the gentlemen he first saw her dancing with, but Shelby was smoother in her dance steps and looked more gorgeous than the first time he laid eyes on her. He decided to ask her to Walk on E. J. Johnson's "It's True (I Love You)." That was so good to him that he asked her to stay with him for the rest of the evening.

Shelby appeared surprised and asked him, "Why do you want me to stay with you for the rest of the evening when you are eyeing Naima?"

He replied, "Because I like you, and I know you like me, too."

She smiled and said, "Yes. That is true. I also love the way you treat me and the ladies."

He wasn't sure what in particular he liked about Shelby. She was the total package, so to speak. Perhaps what he liked most about her was that, like him, she moved in slow motion—never in a hurry to do anything. What he suspected was that she might be freakish although he was not sure of what that might mean in relationship to anything she might do with him or to him. Watching her move her body in space to music that she enjoyed was a wondrous sight, and he inferred and imagined so many things from observing her do that. But he told himself, '*You should leave that alone for the moment.*'

And that is what he did. He took her home that evening and watched her disappear into the high-rise building that she lived in on Michigan Avenue just a little south of 14th Street. They had talked about how each wanted to stay together that evening for whatever they might have been inclined to do, but they had agreed that that might be problematic from the standpoint of its impact on the group. They both seemed to have embraced their phlegmatic perspectives and ways of being in the world and went into a wait-and-see mode.

The next weekend, the group went to see Dave Brubeck at the Symphony Center. Except for Shelby, none of the ladies had attended an event there. They had dinner at Tesori, a restaurant connected to Symphony Center. He had assumed all of the ladies liked jazz and would enjoy the concert, but only Shelby was able to sit through the entire show and enjoy it. The other ladies were up and down in their seats for whatever reason they could find—washroom break, a drink, leg cramps, and even a cigarette outside.

At one point during the concert, Brubeck tells a little story about how when he first started out, he and his group would try to get the audience to be quiet by overpowering them by playing very loud.

"At some gig," he says, "I had a very famous jazz musician pull me aside and say: 'Don't try to overwhelm your audience, make them strain to hear you by playing softly.' It worked, and we have played that way since then."

Instinctively, he and Shelby grabbed one another's hand and did a bit of church, body rocking to signify "amen." Brubeck closed out the evening with his signature piece: "Take Five." Justin thought that he and Shelby seemed to be more in sync at the end of the evening than they had been at the beginning of it. Justin sensed that Naima apparently felt that, too, and to break that off, she had suggested that they go south to hear some real jazz at City Life on 83rd Street just west of Cottage Grove.

As they entered City Life, mostly patronized by locals, they were initially considered as outsiders. Naima, however, broke the ice by saying to the barmaid, "Y'all got some champagne for us to drink." The barmaid and crowd laughed at that because they knew from her appearance that Naima was a city slicker and not a country girl as her speech suggested.

The barmaid replied, "How many bottles and glasses?"

Naima said, "Two bottles and five glasses."

They had been seated on the west side of the bar along a mirrored wall with small tables with three chairs at each one. The second set was starting, and a young saxophonist came out and tore up the place. From what Justin could gather, no one in the group knew quite what to expect regarding music at City Life, but it was wildly better than what they anticipated. Justin checked to see if the group wanted to stay for the third set. When everyone agreed to stay, he ordered catfish and fried chicken wings from the kitchen, which had just announced that it was taking last orders.

All of the ladies lived south of the jazz lounge, except Shelby, so Rachel drove the ladies home, and he took Shelby with him north. When that suggestion had been made in the lounge, the ladies looked at each other, but all agreed that that was what made the most sense. In the car alone with Shelby, he casually reached over and put his hand inside of her bra and gently rubbed one of her breasts that he had been admiring for most of the evening.

He said, "Ok. You got a little something there."

She replied, "You couldn't easily see that?"

His comeback was, "Not as well as I could feel that."

As they entered his apartment, he reached back with his left hand to pull Shelby towards him to dance. Simultaneously, with his right hand, he hit the music icon on his iPhone and the stereo started up with one of his favorite tunes by the Moments, "I Could Have Loved You." He had always loved the way the lead singer would say, "You were right for me, baby," and stretch out the word "right" so that it sounded like "riiiggghhhttt."

Apparently Shelby liked that, too, because she would imitate loudly the singer each time he reached that point in the song and softly fold herself into his arms as if she could stay there forever. He had pushed the repeat function on the iPhone so that the song played over and over again four times.

They had danced and kissed through all four plays of the song, and at the end of the fourth time, he pushed the shuffle function on his phone. He hadn't planned it that way, but The Temptations' "Some

Enchanted Evening" started to play. He got the chilled champagne glasses from the freezer, poured champagne for them to drink, and returned to the couch where Shelby now sat naked.

He had always thought that Shelby was an attractive woman. She had a face that appeared to be a confluence of the faces of Pam Grier and Sofia Loren, and she had a body that appeared to be more perfect than either of those two ladies. Thoughts of statues of Amazon women in the museums of Italy that he had visited as a soldier and other times ran through his mind, and he smiled at the thought of mounting this seemingly unparalleled specimen of the human race and going home to glory.

Shelby was almost six feet tall and weighed one hundred and forty pounds. She had full breasts and shapely hips unblemished by time or childbearing. Her legs were full from the calf to the ankle and had been enhanced by dancing a lot. She had a buttock that was prettier than Felecia's because it was attached to such an imposing body. She also had a smile that was wicked but sincere.

Still fully dressed, he sat next to Shelby as she said: "Before we start anything, I have to tell you something." She had continued before he could respond: "I have a good man who wants to marry me and have kids and stuff like that."

He said to himself, '*Then why are you here naked on my sofa?*'

Shelby continued, "I know you are asking yourself what am I doing here in your apartment?"

He nodded his head a few times to acknowledge her comment. Shelby was sipping the glass of champagne and staring at the tall buildings in the downtown area. She spoke again: "I have watched you over several years, and I have had a crush on you probably all of that time. The gentleman who wants to marry me has been chasing me all that time that I was looking at and yearning for you. You never even looked at me until the night of the Halloween party. The irony of that is I had just told him a few weeks earlier that I would marry him."

Justin fully appreciated her situation, but he still said to her: "At this point in my life, I am not interested in playing in anyone's life, and I sure am not going to let anyone play in mine."

He stared at Shelby, but she did not even blink at his comment. She just stood up and removed his clothes and led him into the bedroom. He sat on the side of the bed while she stood. Alternating one breast at a time, he gently rubbed and sucked her breasts until she started to moan and secrete joy juice down her legs and onto his foot. She kissed him all over his face, put her tongue deep into his mouth, mounted him, and rode quietly home with him in tow.

When he woke up the next morning, Shelby was gone. She left a note saying that she had stayed until the sun came up and was going to take a cab home since it was such a short distance. She thanked him for a great evening and told him she would see him around. He was awake, but he did not want to leave his bed. The scent of Shelby was still on the pillows and sheets, and he wanted to hold onto that as long as he could. He knew he would not have her back in his bed again. In that moment, he was mellow—neither happy nor sad.

CHAPTER TWENTY-THREE

Love Defined

Except to go to work, he did not leave the house for several weeks. Then one late Friday evening, he got a call from Naima inquiring about his whereabouts. She then gave him an invitation to join her and several ladies at a Steppers' set at the Marmon Grand, which was not too far from where he lived. As he dressed to go down to the Marmon Grand, his thoughts were mostly about Shelby and how he might never see her again. It was a mystery to him how she had been in his orbit for several years and for him not to have taken notice of her. He sort of knew how that worked—it was all a matter of focusing.

When he entered the Marmon Grand, the place was packed, and he thought about the crowds he had seen at the Peps: A rich mixture of Black folks from all strata of the Black community. Several fellows wore red outfits—suit, shoes, socks, hat, and tie. One fellow's red outfit looked gaudy, but a couple of other fellows looked quite elegant in their red outfits. So it wasn't the color of your outfit that made you get the label of "bad" (meaning good) or "bad" (meaning not good). Rather, it was things like the shade of red, cut of the suit, the way the suit hung on your body, the accessories you had matched with the suit, on so on.

In contrast, to the fellows in red outfits and other vibrant colors were the fellows in double-breasted designers suits of various hues. He was in the latter group with a black Joseph Abboud suit with a subtle pattern you could only see if you were viewing it from as close as a few inches. As usual, he had put on a white shirt and added to that a Sean John's black and white tie that also had a subtle pattern. To get a little kick to his outfit, he stuck a white handkerchief in the pocket of his suit coat, which always made him think of the outfits worn by men in the black and white movies that he still loved to watch.

While he stood in line at the bar to get a drink, someone had taken his hand and was pulling him towards the dance floor to Step to Nicolas Bearde's "Can We Pretend." He was shortly able to see that it was Shelby who wanted to Step to one of the "baddest" Stepping pieces around.

As he fully took her in, he realized more consciously that Shelby's taste in clothes was always simple and elegant. It made him think about women in pictures he had seen of his older brothers and the women they were fond of hanging with. This night she had on some kind of lilac, tight fitting dress that was above her knees in length. It was also off the shoulders and had some added material at the waist.

They had only made a few moves on the dance floor before he was thinking: '*She came to dance tonight.*' He usually had a predilection to go back and forth between Bopping and Stepping whenever he was on the dance floor, but this night he was strictly in the Stepping mode. In a move he had practiced many times before, he decided to rock his upper body left and right, a move he had picked up a long time ago from a friend of his first wife. He continued to Step by moving his feet back and forth with subtle kicks, sometimes in a six-beat count and other times in an eight-beat count.

Shelby smiled at his antics and then put her moves on automatic pilot. He knew that he could not consciously keep up with her, so he went on automatic pilot, too. In a move he had not done or practiced, he found himself stepping back on his left foot and then rocking forward and backward on that foot in the way that he had rocked from side to side in another of his moves. Shelby kept up and by the time the song ended, he was euphoric; and they both held one another as they left the floor talking and laughing.

He knew that if someone had asked them to duplicate some of their moves made on the floor that night, they would not have been able to do so. He felt that a dancing high is one of those highs you cannot get any other way. The music, the liquor, the lights, the crowd, the setting, the movement of your partner's body, and your own movement in space; all make for improvisational moments that approach those of jazz musicians who often cannot repeat a bit of magic that was theirs for only a night or part of a night or part of an hour.

Shelby asked to go home with him that night, but he told her that was not possible.

She asked, "Why is that not possible?"

He replied, "Because it would not be good for you or me. You seem to be on a path that takes you where you want to be in life. Stay on the path."

At that point, Naima came up and asked him to dance on Jerry Butler's "I Dig You Baby."

He thought she wanted to Step, but she said, "I want you to hold me close. Let's Walk."

He was glad Naima had asked him to dance. He knew that a few seconds more of looking into Shelby's face and taking in her lovely body in that stunning dress would have taken away his ability not to honor her request to be with him in his place and his bed. Naima held his attention through the first song, but when the DJ played Eddie Kendrick's "Tell Her Love Has Felt The Need," his eyes became watery.

He thought, '*I would have wanted to dance with Shelby on this one. It says what I so curtly said to her. I wish I had that other moment back and could dance with her now.*'

Naima seemed to have sensed that something was not quite right, so she stopped dancing in the middle of the record, held his hand gently, left the dance floor, and said: "Buy me a drink."

After they had a drink in hand and sat comfortably on a couch in an area outside of the ballroom, Naima said: "You want to talk about it?"

He surprised her and himself when he said: "Yes."

Never one to talk easily about what he was feeling, he decided he felt comfortable enough with Naima to discuss with her his relationship with another woman. He started by saying, "Shelby wants to be with me, but she still wants to go ahead with her plans to be married and all that other stuff that follows. Why not just go do what she is inclined to do and leave the other bullshit alone?"

Naima put her hand over her mouth to hide the broad smile on her face. She then said, "You really don't get it, do you?"

He stared at her face to see if he could discern some meaning from that that was not coming from the words she spoke. Then he said: "I guess I don't."

She pulled him closer and said: "The ladies see you as Iceberg Slim, Darcy, Casanova, Don Juan, Don 'Magic' Juan, and a host of other male seducers. You are the ladies' male counterpart! At least you are an alter ego of them."

He waited for her to continue. "Most women see themselves as the ultimate in lovers or seducers rivaling, in general, nymphs and sirens; in particular, Cleopatra, Catherine the Great, Scarlet O'Hara, and so on. You will always be deeply loved by women, but in the end, you will always be loved mostly from afar."

He shuddered at her words but continued to stare at her beautiful face. With just a little hesitation in his move, he took Naima's hand and said: "Come and go home with me tonight." This time, it was she who shuddered.

With no hesitation in her response, she said: "Yes."

For some months, since he first held her close and moved smoothly to music by the Whispers at the gala, he wanted to embrace Naima and tell her about his feelings for her that began the first time he saw her in the dance club with Rachel. In reference to what she had just told him, he felt that she knew what she was talking about because she appeared to be a personification of the archetypical women she had just described. He again shuddered at the thought, and his instinct was to run.

She again seemed to have sensed the moment and said: "You are afraid of me, aren't you?"

He replied, "Yes. In a way I am, but not in the way you mean. In the usual sense of that word, I am not afraid of any man, woman, or beast."

She laughed at his bravado, and said, "We shall see."

As they sat staring intently at one another, Shelby, Rachel, and Mattie approached them, and Shelby said, "It's still early. Let's go to CloseUp2 and have a nightcap."

They all agreed that that was a good idea.

When they reached CloseUp2 on south Clark Street in the South Loop area, they all piled out of Shelby's Mercedes-Benz sedan. He had been in the front seat with Shelby and felt his obligation was to hold her hand and the hand of Naima. Rachel and Mattie grabbed the free hand of Shelby and Naima.

That is how they entered the club, almost pulling one another like cars on a train—with Rachel in the lead. As they entered the club, virtually every person in the bar stared at them, including the bartender and owner.

The owner, Jimmy, greeted them all with a hug and said to Justin: "Hey man, I haven't seen you in awhile. Who are these lovely ladies?"

Justin introduced each of the ladies who got a thorough visual examination from Jimmy, who stared with a lechery Justin had not seen before from him.

Jimmy then said, "We have a full house tonight. Maysa is appearing here this evening. Let me see if I find can a few dudes to give up four seats at the bar. Do you mind standing, Justin?"

To which he responded: "No. Not at all." With little noticeable commotion, the ladies had seats at the bar and were shortly after that sipping champagne.

Jimmy told him that Maysa was on some promotional tour, so she was not scheduled to perform at the club. However, Jimmy did persuade Maysa to lip-sync two of her songs that he played over the sound system: "What Are You Doing the Rest of Your Life" and "I Put a Spell on You." On the first song, Justin spontaneously grabbed Shelby and gently pulled her to an area of the club that was available for dancing.

She said to him, "Who are you taking home with you?"

He said, "I don't know. At the Marmon Grand, I thought it might be Naima. As I hold you in my arms now, it might be you."

Shelby stopped dancing, looked him in the eyes, and said: "You are such a fucking bullshitter. Why don't you get each of the ladies for part of a record? That might help you make up your mind."

He chose Naima for the second part of "What Are You Doing the Rest of Your Life." He then rotated Rachel and Mattie in on "I Put a Spell on You."

Mattie was one of those ladies with great legs, nice behind, cute face, flowing hair, and mellow persona. She excited a man in some subtle ways that he was sure even she did not know or understand. He impulsively nibbled her on the ear, and her body convulsed for a second.

She said, "Be careful Justin."

He knew she was right, and he said, "I will."

Just then, "Somebody Else's Arms" by Maze started to play. Mattie beckoned to all of the ladies to join them on the floor. He smiled and thought that Stepping with all four of the women on one of his favorite tunes by Maze would be one of those magical moments that life offers only a few times. They all giggled like young schoolgirls dancing at their first sock hop.

He watched them all move synchronously to the sound of Maze and Frankie Beverly's smooth voice and cross-generation soul music. He was able to turn all of the ladies as a group and as individuals. He knew how to dance with two ladies at the same time, but dancing with four ladies at the same time was a "second" for him and them.

Justin noticed that the entire club was now watching their antics, and he knew that the odds being waged among the crowd were that they had practiced dancing together before this moment. To keep them going, the club owner played another Maze tune, "Call On Me." At that point, half of the club was up and dancing. The moment was reminiscent of a ballet show, except it was the audience doing the dancing while the ballet dancers watched.

He had seen each lady's legs, but he had not seen all of their legs together in motion from a single vantage point in such short dresses. He could conjure no words to either describe what he saw or what he felt. But he was sure the moment would always be somewhere in the recesses of his mind, so he just flowed with the moment without trying to capture or hold on to it.

He was so totally enraptured that he was still moving hypnotically with the ladies when Earth, Wind, and Fire's "Cruising" started to play. The ladies all seemed to be prancing at that point, and he thought to himself, '*I have made my transition with my angels at my side!*'

He found himself at the bar sandwiched between the ladies: Shelby and Naima immediately to his left and right; Rachel and Mattie were one person over on each side. They were apparently just as high as he was because they were all leaning into the center to make sure they were part of any exchange that took place.

From behind the bar, Jimmy slapped his hand and introduced him to the bartender: "Justin this is Brian. Whenever you come in, he will make sure you and the ladies have what you need."

Naima said, "I am hungry, I need food. Where can we eat Justin?"

He replied, "At this hour there are only three places I know that are still open. One is not too far from here on Roosevelt and Canal called White Palace Grill. The other two are up north not too far from here. One is Bijan's Bistro that is around 600 North State. The other is Tempo around 900 North State. What's your pleasure?"

Naima said, "You choose."

He said, "Ok. Bijan. I like the late-night café atmosphere of Bijan. Parking may be difficult, but at this hour, it probably will not be. Let's go!"

Shelby said to Justin, "Since you know where we are headed, why don't you drive?"

He put out his hand as a response to Shelby's request and said to himself: '*God you are so fine. I wish I knew how to keep you in my life—at least for a while.*'

As if she had heard him, she deliberately got in front of him and switched a bit. Naima saw her and said: "Stop it, girl!" They all laughed at that bit of shenanigans by Shelby.

Bijan's was more crowded than he had anticipated. But the maître d' recognized him and pointed to a table near an area that opened to the outside during the summer. Mattie, the quiet one, said, "That's what I'm talking about." As they sat and ate and talked and felt the warm Chicago summer breeze wash across their bodies in the early morning hours, each of them appeared to be in a tranquil state: free of any envy, jealousy, or competitive feelings about who would ultimately be able to do what with whom.

He so enjoyed the outing; he said: "Let's all spend the evening at my place. Y'all can have the bed and couch. I will sleep on the floor."

All thumbs went up on that suggestion.

CHAPTER TWENTY-FOUR

Wild Is the Wind

Justin felt that that tranquil state that came over the group on their first visit to Bijan's took up residence in the group for the next year and a half. Shortly after their visit to Bijan's, they had outings together three or four times a week. Initially, they would just get together at Steppers' sets held at the Marmon Grand, Room 43, The Grand Ballroom, The Legacy, and other clubs in the city. Because those parties often ended too soon in the evening, they added to their street running a visit to CloseUp2 several nights a week, usually starting on Wednesday night.

Some weeks they would start on Wednesday night and run the streets together for the next five or six nights in a row. To add a little variety to their gatherings, they often found something special to do. Some nights it was a movie and dinner. Other nights it was dinner and a play. They saw almost all of August Wilson's plays: "Two Trains Running," "The Piano Lesson," "Seven Guitars," "Ma Rainey's Black Bottom," "King Hedley II," "Joe Turner's Come and Gone," "Jitney," "Gem of the Ocean," and "Fences."

Another of the "something special to do" was jazz concerts and jazz sets around the city. One summer, within a two-month period and in various settings, they saw: Sonny Rollins and McCoy Tyner at Symphony Center; Sun Ra and Ahmad Jamal at summer concerts at the South Shore Cultural Center; George Benson and Al Jarreau at Northerly Island on the lakefront; Pharoah Sanders at the African Festival of the Arts in Washington Park; and Dee Alexander at the Chicago Jazz Festival on the lakefront.

Some days they would start with dinner; do an early jazz set somewhere; do a Steppers' set; go to CloseUp2 for another jazz set; go to Red's on Stony Island for a late evening jam session; have breakfast at the closest late-hour restaurant; and then go to Justin's place to drink more champagne and sit on the patio and watch the sun come up. On one of those mornings when the sun appeared on the horizon over the lake, all of the ladies except one decided to go home that Sunday morning to get ready for church.

Naima feigned being too sleepy and drunk to leave, and several ladies carried her up to Justin's apartment and laid her on the couch in his living room. He was fine with that, and he told the other ladies to leave her there until she felt well enough to go home. He embraced each lady at the door and went immediately to bed. At one point, he heard himself snoring and awoke to Naima's massage of his behind and genitals. Neither spoke as they rolled over to face one another. They gently embraced and copulated effortlessly. He had not even thought about making love to Naima, at least that evening, but he did wonder how he had resisted both the thought and the act for so long.

Apparently something they both had wanted badly, they made love in almost every nook and cranny of his apartment that was comfortable. He was amazed at their stamina, and they howled and laughed and cried until the late afternoon when they both appeared to be feeling hungry and exhausted.

She spoke first: "Was that as good as you expected?"

Trying to discern her mood, he said: "Yes. But you knew it would be."

Her reply was, "Yes. Even though I have only been with fewer than the number of men I can count on one hand, I have mastered the art of loving."

He knew that was a lie, especially the first part of her story, but he had to agree without equivocation with the second part of it. He wanted to ask her about a particular number of men she had been with, but he decided not to fool with the apparent chemistry that existed between them.

Instead, he said, "Where is your husband?"

She told him that her husband was a musician who traveled a lot and was presently in Germany touring. She added, "But he left me two years ago to be with a White woman that he met in Stuttgart, Germany. So I have lived alone for several years."

His immediate response was to feel sorry for Naima; but shortly after that, he knew that she was fine. From what he could observe and had been told, Naima was a strong, Black woman who liked having a man around, but she did not have to have one around, at least not on any all-the-time basis. She had been married twice, had two boys, finished college, owned five businesses, bought and sold three homes, been around the world twice, and gone back to work for a non-profit organization after retiring from the United States Postal Service after 30 years.

Still relatively young, in her late 50's, she had told him that she had decided that this time in her life was her time—to see the world as she pleased, to do what she wanted, and to be with any person she thought could bring her the most pleasure—intellectually, emotionally, and sexually.

As good as that time together was for the next two years and six months, both he and Naima knew that what they had was not meant to be forever. Deep down in her soul, Naima wanted to return to her husband. Deep down in his soul, Justin knew he had to finish his journey to learn how to speak to his soul.

Over the period that they saw one another, they had unwittingly rehearsed their ultimate breakup by not being in contact for months at a time. Then, on several occasions, they would just suddenly be back in each other's life, arms, and bed as if they had never separated.

So one late evening as Naima prepared to go home after one of their best sessions of lovemaking, Naima announced that her husband had heard about her affair with him and wanted her to come to Europe to join him on his tour there for the next six months. She said, "I know what this is about, but I still want to join him in Europe; for a lot of different reasons. Please say you understand."

He felt a little sick to his stomach, but he still managed to get out, "I do. I wish you love, and I wish you well." He then grabbed his iPhone and played Gloria Lynne's "I Wish You Love." Naima, at first, thought he was trying to play with her or hurt her, but she looked into his face and eyes and saw the tears well up. The expression on his face revealed how deeply he loved her and how much he wished her love.

She pulled him towards her, and they quietly sobbed for the length of the entire record. He then hit another tune on his iPhone: "I Wish You Well" by Frankie Beverly and Maze. This time, he was the one who did the pulling. As they started to Step so lightly and sweetly that tears welled up in her eyes, she told him: "I won't go if you marry me."

He opened his mouth to say that he would marry her if she stayed; but before the words could come out, images of Scottie, April and Haley appeared in his head. He was unable to say the words, and Naima let his hand go. She went to the closet near the front door, put on her coat, and left without saying goodbye. He was tempted to run after her but recognized immediately that this was one of those times to not pursue beyond the moment. He wasn't sure what to do after Naima closed the door, so he got a Kahlua and cream drink and put the Moments' "I Could Have Loved You" on repeat mode on his iPhone.

CHAPTER TWENTY-FIVE

Finding Love Again

Naima called two weeks later to tell him that she was on her way to Europe to join her husband. She sounded good on the phone; and he was tempted to beg her to stay. He knew, however, that would be too little too late. Instead, he told her how much he would miss her, and again wished her love and wished her well.

She jokingly said, "You had your chance, boy."

They both laughed, and just said, "Bye."

After speaking with Naima, he dressed and headed out the door to CloseUp2. His heart was heavy and his stomach in a knot, and he knew that staying at home alone was not the thing to do. Since CloseUp2 was only a few blocks from his place and it was summer in Chicago, he decided to walk that half-mile.

The owner, Jimmy, greeted him warmly as he entered the place. He was offered a seat at the bar next to a lady who was rather cute.

He offered to buy her a drink, and she offered, "My name is Cecilia. I work downtown and live not too far from here with my daughter."

From that point, the conversation was all over the place, and late in the evening, he offered to take her to breakfast at Bijan's. After they had eaten, he dropped her at her place and told the cabdriver to take him back to CloseUp2.

For the next six months, he ran the streets like a mad dog. One lady that he met acted like a mad dog each of several times that they met, so he decided to leave her alone. He repeated the CloseUp2 scene with other single ladies, pairs of ladies, and groups of ladies: A little conversation, a few drinks, and breakfast at Bijan's early in the morning.

Nothing was working for him at this point. Just when he was inclined to get off the party and dating scene for a while, he met again a young lady that he had dated some time ago. Fifteen years ago, they had dated for about a year, but she had four kids and a husband who was a state trooper. She and her husband had been separated when they were dating, but he still felt too many constraints in that relationship.

When he saw Donna, this time, he was immediately struck by her mature, beautiful look. She had gotten a little bigger, but even that made her look better than what he recalled. She was now divorced, and all of her children, except one, were out of the house.

As much as he tried, he could not make a go of that relationship: Donna was a fabulous woman to look at, but her conversation was only about matters of the day, and her dance moves did not come near to what he was accustomed to. She was good in the bed, but there was no subtlety to her lovemaking. That encounter lasted about four months. Without any conversation about it, they both just stopped calling one another.

He had not been out for about a month when he decided to go the Marmon Grand for a Wednesday night set. He had fun that evening dancing, and he was glad that he had decided to come out for the evening. Late in the evening, as the crowd thinned, he saw a shapely young lady in a cute dress dancing with a dude he knew. So he walked up to the couple as they continued to dance and hollered, "I am next!" He then pointed to the young lady and then to himself. She smiled and nodded her head.

As they danced, she introduced herself as Lisa. He thought to himself, "Cute name. Cute dress. Cute legs. Nice moves. Nice behind!" They had Stepped on Eloise Law's "The Last Days of Summer," and he was surprised when the DJ followed that with "Love Comes Easy" by the same artist. Lisa was small in some ways, so he wrapped both arms around her waist and started to Walk.

She said she did not know how to Walk, but she wanted to learn. The first steps she made were tentative, but he told her: "Lean your body in on mine and go with the flow of the music and my moves." That worked. If you didn't know better, you would have bet money that she knew how to Walk before that night.

Lisa was just what he had been looking for. She had a lot of style in terms of dress—probably as good as some women he had known and a lot better than others he had known. She had a decent conversation. She could dance. And she had style regarding manners and mannerisms.

He asked her out on some occasion that required a date; she said she wanted to join him, but she had already made a commitment to a friend who might come to town during the same period of time he was asking about. She said she would let him know in a few days.

She was unable to go with him on that date, but she did commit to a party that they both dressed up for. She was lovely that evening, and he was spiffy looking. They went to a second party the same evening, and he could only think about how lovely she looked and how graceful she moved about the room. He took her home that evening, and only pecked her on the cheek. He watched her go into a building in the Lake Meadows complex and waited until she waved from her window on the 10th floor.

They hung tough for several months without even an attempt to be intimate. They went to concerts, Steppers' sets, picnics, and other events. They also ate at some of the best restaurants in the city. On one occasion they went to Table Fifty-Two, the restaurant owned by Oprah's ex-personal chef, Art Smith. It was winter in Chicago, and when she picked him up, he could only see the beautiful little black coat she wore. When they got inside the restaurant, she removed the coat and revealed a stunning little black dress that accentuated all of her curves and displayed her gorgeous legs.

He was impressed. Apparently so was the maître de who offered a table with subdued lighting and lots of space. The food that evening was as good as advertised, perhaps better. The conversation was good and was lighthearted. They liked one another, and they both felt that.

At one point in the evening, the waitress said: "I can tell you both like each other. You are a handsome couple. That's the nicest little black dress that I have ever seen, and the gentleman's outfit, especially that tie, is gorgeous and complement's the lady's outfit. Dessert is on me." He, too, liked the tie he had worn that evening—a black and deep tan paisley tie by Sean John, another of his favorite designers.

After dinner, they drove down Lake Shore Drive so they could see the city in all of its glory. They went back to his place, but he had already decided to leave her alone—at least for the moment. She left his place at about 1:00 A.M., and told him she would be able to make it home without help from him since she had moved to a location on Michigan Avenue in a high-rise that had indoor, secure parking. They hugged for a long time at the door, and he watched her move in slow motion down the hall to the elevator. She turned, threw him a kiss, and got into the elevator.

He felt so good about the evening; he was already planning where and when they might next get together. Before he could get in bed, she had called to tell him that she was in and would talk to him tomorrow. He was gleeful about the way the evening turned out, but as he turned on his side to go to sleep, there was a bit of a disease, as that term was originally defined—lack of ease, in his soul. He ignored that and fell asleep after a few minutes.

The next day, he called her in the early afternoon to ask if she wanted to meet him at a Steppers' party at the Grand Ballroom that evening. She said yes, and she told him she would call him back at around 5:00 P.M. By the time 5:00 P.M. had come and gone, he got a little concerned but decided to give her until 6:00 P.M. At 6:10, he called, and she answered. She told him that her sister had called and asked her to go to a party with her. So she was going to do that instead of going with him to the Grand Ballroom.

He wasn't sure why she did not feel a need to communicate that to him prior to his calling, but he left that alone and just said, "Ok." He started to stay in for the evening, but since he was already dressed based upon their earlier conversation, he called a taxi and headed to the Grand Ballroom.

He had no sooner stepped in the door before he saw her leaning in between the legs of a dude that she had told him about. They had talked about her relationship with the other dude, so he wasn't concerned or mad about what he saw at that moment in that regard. What he didn't understand was why she had lied about what she would be doing for the evening.

After a short while, he asked Lisa to dance. Not too long into the dance, he asked about why she had lied, and she said, "I don't want to talk about that now! I will call you later to talk about that." With that, she abruptly turned to leave in the middle of the song. He reflexively grabbed her by the arm, perhaps too tight; and he then realized that he was about to make a scene, so he let her go.

He just walked out of the place without acknowledging her or anyone else. He hailed a taxi and told the driver to take him to CloseUp2. Before the taxi had driven one block, he received a text from Lisa saying that she would call him the next day.

His reply was simple: "Fuck you!"

Chapter Twenty-Six

I'm Glad There Is You

In the next few months after the almost-affair with Lisa, he just partied and went solo to events of various kinds. His barber, who was also a stylist, had hinted at some ladies that she knew who were looking for a good man. Initially, he just laughed and did not respond. Then on one visit to the shop, he said, "Give me a name and a number." Brenda gave him the name of a woman who was a partner in a law firm in downtown Chicago. A few days later, he gave that same woman a call but got no answer. He left a message but got no return call. Always one to give a person the benefit of the doubt, he called the woman again with the same results.

When he saw his barber, Brenda, several weeks later, she was styling the hair of a woman he had seen in the shop many times over the years—probably three decades. They had acknowledged each other with a nod over those many decades but had not spoke. His barber started to tell the woman, Janet, about him and how he had failed to call the woman whose name and number she had given him. The barber intentionally talked loud enough for him to hear, and he thought that Janet was the woman that he had tried to call.

He explained to Brenda and Janet that he had called twice and got no answer. He also told them that he had not gotten a call back although he had left his cell and home numbers. As he stood in front of the two women trying to explain to them that he was a man of his word, it occurred to him that perhaps he did not have the right telephone number of the woman he was calling. Brenda had written the name and number of the woman down for him, so he asked her to check the number. Sure enough, she had transposed two of the numbers she had written down.

Eager to remedy a situation not of his making, he offered his card to Janet. Initially, she did not want to take it and said, "Oh. I am not the woman whose name and number Brenda gave you."

His reply was, "That's ok. Take my card anyway, and give me your card."

She took his card and handed him one of her cards. He looked at the card and said, "There is no home number on here. Would you write that on the back." Again she acquiesced. He turned to Brenda and said: "See. That was your fault I did not contact the woman."

Brenda just said, "Get on out of here."

All three of them laughed, and he sat down to wait for his turn in the chair.

He glanced at Janet when she got up to sit under the dryer. She had on jeans, but they were tight enough to reveal a nice behind and shapely legs. He could also see that her breasts were ample if not huge. She had a face that was really cute and inviting, especially when she smiled. She moved gracefully in the space of the shop.

She was finished before he had an opportunity to have Brenda start on him. And after she picked up her purse and paid Brenda, he stood up and assumed a pose that suggested something that Janet seemed not to understand because she just stared at him.

He then said: "Can you dance?"

Janet said, "Yes."

He said, "Let me see how good you are."

There was always music playing in the shop, but he was almost ecstatic when the Joy Tones' "This Love That I'm Giving You" started to play at the same time that he had struck a pose to ask Janet to dance with him. She made claims about being able to Bop but not being able to Step. He was impressed, however, with what she was able to do. She was like him, and moved in and out of Stepping—some Stepping moves alternating with Bopping moves. In addition, at various points, she had this wiggle of her behind that told him that he ought to at least take her out to dinner.

The next day he made reservations for dinner at Gioco, a nice little Italian restaurant in the South Loop. He had not talked with Janet, but he called her shortly after he had made the reservation. She wasn't home.

He left a message: "I have made dinner reservations for two at a restaurant called Gioco. Would you be kind enough to join me in a conversation over dinner this evening? Give me a callback."

At around 5:00 P.M. he had not heard from Janet, and he called the restaurant to cancel the dinner reservations.

Twenty minutes later, Janet called to tell him that she would love to join him in a conversation over dinner. He told her he had not heard from her, so he had canceled the reservations.

He added, "But let me see if I can get the reservations back. I will call you right back."

He was able to get the reservations back. When he called and told her that, they both laughed because both sort of believed in the notion of fate. He told her to meet him at the restaurant and to valet park, for which he would pick up the tab.

He got to the restaurant a little ahead of 7:00 P.M. to make sure that it was still as nice as he had remembered. It was, and he just took a seat at the bar and ordered a glass of champagne. The bartender told him that they only served an Italian sparkling white wine called prosecco. He quickly said, "That's good."

Janet drove up shortly after he had gotten his drink. He got up and went to the door to greet her, embraced her as she walked in, took her coat and checked it, and invited her to either have a drink at the bar or go straight to their table for dinner. She replied that she was hungry. So he said to the hostess, "We would like to be seated for dinner now."

The waitress took them to an intimate area of the restaurant and put them at a table for two. He held her seat and made sure she was comfortable before he sat down. Janet's hair, now mostly salt and pepper around the edges and almost totally gray on top, looked great. Brenda had done an exceptional job with her hair. Since he sat directly across from her, he now had a view of her pretty face that made him want to kiss her. He resisted that urge. Instead, he made an inquiry about what she might like to drink. She chose to have the prosecco after tasting his.

He smiled at her being comfortable with him right out of the box. He raised his right hand to get the attention of the waiter and ordered a drink for her. He then reached into a small bag that he was holding and gave her a copy of his book that he had published two years earlier. She read the title out loud: "*An Infinity of Interpretations: A Bit Of*

Social Commentary On And A Philosophical Examination Of Life In These Times."

She laughed after she had read the title, and she said: "That's a mouth full for a title. How did you come up with that?"

He tried to explain to her how in graduate school he came across so many different interpretations of the same facts and events described in a variety of courses that he took in a variety of disciplines: history, sociology, psychology, economics, anthropology, geography, and political science. He also told her while that notion of different interpretations of the same facts and events was especially true in the social sciences and humanities; it was also true in the sciences, too.

She leaned forward and said, "Without having read your book, my first question to you is related to your title. Shouldn't the first part of the title be just Infinity of Interpretations since adding the "an" seems to be unnecessary or redundant? I say that because I think of infinity as being singular. There can only be one "infinity" if we think of it in relationship to our present cosmology. Or perhaps you should have just said "An Infinite Number of Interpretations."

He smiled at her jumping right into a conversation at that level of abstraction and thoughtfulness. He replied, "You may be right, but let me make sure I understand what you just said. First, explain to me what you mean by our "present cosmology." She then launched into a short explanation of the Big Bang theory and the relationship of the word infinity to that. She finally said, "So if there is only one universe, there can only be one infinity to speak of."

He licked his lips and smiled again. "Let's assume," he started, "that there is more than one universe. Can we then have more than one infinity?" It was her turn to lick her lips and smile.

Now displaying a full-fledged grin, she sat back farther in her chair and said: "Good response. But I am talking about probability here and not possibility." He laughed because in his mind what he had offered was as probable as it was possible. However, he knew exactly what she was saying.

After that exchange, they decided to get another glass of prosecco and order dinner. He got the fettuccine, and she got grilled salmon. They ordered a salad to share. The waitress quickly brought bread and seasoned olive oil to hold them until the food arrived.

She started the conversation again by saying, "Before we get back to our engaging discussion about your book, let me tell you a little about me and what I know about you. I have watched you over several decades at the shop, and when Scottie mentioned your name to me in a casual conversation some years ago, I knew immediately to whom she had surrendered her soul.

Over the years, I am the one who emboldened Scottie, April, and Haley to help you in learning to speak to your soul. I have to tell you that it was reciprocal because I was emboldened by what they said about you. I have also seen you out at many Steppers' sets and parties over the years, but I never allowed myself to intrude into your world or space."

He was speechless at first. Finally, he said: "Why didn't you just help me yourself?"

She replied, "I was in a bad situation, specifically, a bad marriage. I would not have been able to be with you in the way that Scottie, April, and Haley were with you. I, too, am from Antigua, and the women there, it is believed, can only reach their full potential as human beings by helping a man to learn how to speak to his soul. Don't think, however, that that is a one-way street. What the man has to be able to do in return is to help the woman learn to speak to her soul!"

He nodded his head several times because he knew what she meant. He just stared into her lovely face for a few minutes without speaking.

The waiter brought their food, and they sat and ate in silence. Each understood that they were both trying to take in all of things that had happened to each of them in that moment and over the past three decades when they were not together physically but still in contact with one another either through other individuals or their own spirits touching base each time they saw each other in the shop and nodded but never spoke.

She finally said, "What is the book about that you are now writing?"

He started to ask how did she know that he was now writing a book. He quickly realized how shallow a question that would be.

He told her that his next book, at a certain level, was about life in general and relationships—especially relationships between men and women.

She laughed and said: "You know who you are talking to, right?"

He laughed, picked up his glass, and offered a toast: "To me learning how to speak to my soul and you learning how to speak to yours. I really like you, girl."

Printed in the United States
By Bookmasters